Dennis Apperly was born in Gloucester, England on December 12, 1945. He entered journalism in 1968 in South Africa as a sub-editor/reporter on the South African Press Association in Johannesburg. When he returned to the United Kingdom in early 1970, he embarked upon a career of journalism that lasted for more than 50 years, travelling all over the world in a variety of roles. He became launch editor of the *Gloucester Express* in 1985, when he ran the award-winning Aid Africa Campaign, himself escorting a lorryload of educational supplies to a remote community in Darfur, Sudan, during a civil war in that country. Dennis has worked for a number of newspapers, including the *Bristol Evening Post* and the *Birmingham Post*, and ended his journalistic career as a freelance crime reporter.

When he retired Dennis wrote nine fiction novels and one non-fiction, *The Road to Umm Keddada*. He has had *Wasteground* and *Looking for Lady* published, and the other works are awaiting publication. He has also written numerous poems and essays. Dennis has one son, Laurence and two grandchildren, Molly and Ezra.

Dennis Apperly

Us

AUSTIN MACAULEY PUBLISHERS®

LONDON • CAMBRIDGE • NEW YORK • SHARJAH

A CIP catalogue record for this title is available from the British Library.

ISBN 9781035868209 (Paperback)
ISBN 9781035868216 (Hardback)
ISBN 9781035868223 (ePub e-book)

www.austinmacauley.com

First Published 2024
Austin Macauley Publishers Ltd®
1 Canada Square
Canary Wharf
London
E14 5AA

20240824

Company

I walked alone,
My spirit with the night,
My soul lost to its starry mystery,
And as I looked
Up at each speck of light,
Somewhere some other eyes looked up at me.

1

John Carter narrowed his eyes to a sudden, sharp blast of icy air and turned up his jacket collar. He walked down the steep gangway and eyed the cold March sun disapprovingly as it rose over Heathrow Airport, soon to be closed to tourists.

He was back in the United Kingdom, away from the hustle and bustle of the world, after two long and often uncomfortable years. He was (he managed a wry smile) back 'home'.

Carter walked across the apron to the waiting shuttle bus and joined the crowds of fellow passengers fighting for seats. He did not fight very hard and had to stand. But it was not far and fractionally better that making the short journey by foot.

He stood resignedly at the back of a ragged queue with his forged passport at the ready, and waited for some movement. And after about half an hour of shuffling forward, it was his turn. He tried an apologetic smile to the seated, unsmiling official, passed over his passport and waited. The unsmiling official flicked through the pages, shot Carter a distasteful and speedy appraisal, stamped the passport venomously and handed it back without looking at him.

"Thank you," said Carter pointedly.

"Next," replied the unsmiling official, bending his head to look past Carter. Shaking his head to mark the rudeness,

Carter made off for the carousel to await his luggage—two, bright red suitcases. They were hideous but Carter reckoned rightly that nobody else would buy such ugly things and so it would make identification simple, which it always did.

He soon picked up the two suitcases and walked off to the exit doors and to the fresh air.

"Where to, Mister?" asked the taxi-driver.

"To the Hilton," said Carter with an air of bravado, which the taxi-driver noted.

"Righto, Mister," said the taxi-driver. Having noticed Carter's rather drab and obviously cheap clothes, he added, "And I suppose the company are paying, Mister." No 'sir' but just plain 'Mister'. Carter shrugged (although the taxi-driver could not see) and he said nothing. It had been, after all, a long day. And a bed was all he wanted.

About an hour later, he checked into the hotel and, after dumping his two cases in the room, he made a beeline for the bar. It was empty apart from a woman sitting on a stool. Carter joined her, a couple of stools away, and ordered a whisky and water with three cubes of ice. She caught his eye and he smiled. She smiled back.

"Had a long day?" she said after noticing his crumpled clothes and the tired look in the eyes. He nodded and gulped at his whisky greedily and then closed his eyes and gave a deep sigh.

The woman sipped at her drink, some sort of cocktail, put her head to one side and said: "Have you come far?" He opened his eyes, looked at the woman closely, noticed the friendly smile on her lips, took in her long, dark hair, great figure and beautiful face and nodded again.

"Australia. A long, long flight."

"Qantas?"

"Yes, yes, of course. But it seemed to take forever." He shook his head, took a more cautious sip of his whisky, moved off his stool and sat down next to her.

"You don't mind, do you?" he asked, knowing the answer. And the woman shook her head and smiled, rearranging herself for the conversation to come.

"And you…" Carter trailed. "Where are you off to?"

"Cheltenham, for the Gold Cup race meeting tomorrow. Catching the coach from Victoria Coach Station."

Carter started. He put down his whisky and scratched the back of his head. "So am I," he said. "I live there. Well, small world isn't it. Have you been to the festival before?"

"No, no," she replied and added a shade resignedly: "It's for a feature I've been asked to write. Sort of colour piece about what happens behind the scenes, so to speak. Have to talk to some pretty boring people. Never mind, it's a job."

Carter made a sudden decision, finished his drink and stood up.

"I will see you tomorrow, okay? We can share the same taxi." He shook her hand, treated her to a warm smile and walked away. A sudden thought occurred to him and he turned around and said: "Oh by the way, what is your name?"

"Christine," she replied. "Christine Jackson. See you tomorrow, after breakfast, at about ten. Is that okay with you?"

"Okay… at about ten," he said.

Staggering with the clumsy weight of two bright red suitcases Carter took the lift to his third-floor room and, once inside, flopped onto the bed and stared at the ceiling with unseeing eyes. When he closed them, Christine's face swam up: brown eyes, large eyes, looking straight back at him; the lips were slightly parted and she was smiling. He opened his eyes wide and shook his head to rid himself of the image. It was a strange, unfamiliar feeling he had and he shivered and it was not from the cold. He sprang to his feet, strode across the room to a drinks cabinet, made himself a whisky and water and some ice from the fridge and sat down on the armchair that overlooked the window. He thought about the future: his return to Cheltenham and his ultimate return home in a few weeks' time.

Carter got to his feet, walked across the room and turned on the television, returning to the armchair. After a few seconds the picture appeared: it was a piece about the Cheltenham Festival, the hopefuls, a potted history and a few celebs. It was loud, flustered and silly, but Carter settled back in his armchair to take in the nonsense. It was just what he needed… and it was his 'hometown' after all.

Along came the adverts and Carter closed his eyes until they were over. He wished he could close his ears too but his earthly body said no. And so he waited. Only two words from the female presenter made him open his eyes and sit up straight.

"Christine Jackson, the well-known *Times* feature writer and campaigner, will be joining us tomorrow afternoon, so make sure you don't miss what promises to be a lively debate," shouted a bubbly presenter.

"That's where I shall be," said Carter to the wall. But the wall did not answer, so he settled back in his armchair, took a hefty gulp of his whisky and continued to watch the tiresome scene-setter.

One word puzzled him: campaigner. What did she campaign about and why didn't the presenter explain? It must be a well-known cause, a cause that everyone already knew about. Carter found himself smiling, a secretive smile, and he then frowned as an alien emotion crept into his mind: curiosity and nothing to do with fact-finding.

Two whiskies—and large ones—and two hours later, he staggered to his feet, turned off the television and went to bed, where he slept like a baby.

For the first time in his life, he dreamed and it disturbed him. He woke up several times, breathless and disorientated, and waited to go back to sleep again. It was always the same dream: Christine Jackson, riding a horse, her long hair fluttering in the wind, and laughing. She was always riding away from him, looking over her shoulder. He slept very little that night.

****

He saw her at breakfast but she was the other side of the dining room and so he left her to it. She had seen him too and made the same decision. She got up to go while he was still making a mess of his scrambled eggs.

Carter finished his breakfast, picked up his bright red suitcases and made a beeline for reception, where he ordered a taxi, paid the bill and backed through the swing doors to a glorious, if chilly, morning. There he waited, but not for long. In ten minutes a Hackney cab arrived, black of course. He stood ramrod straight with one hand on the top of the open passenger door and waited for Christine Jackson to make an appearance. Which, after three or four minutes, she did.

"Your carriage awaits," announced Carter imperiously and bowed his head in mock deference. Christine smiled radiantly, acknowledged the bow with a squeeze of his upper arm, leaving her holdall on the pavement for Carter to pick up. They travelled to Victoria Coach Station in comfortable silence.

An hour later, they had boarded the National Express coach, which was almost full of obvious racegoers (their garish clothing gave them away), but they found a couple of seats near the back. Carter settled back and closed his eyes while Christine looked excitedly out of the window as the coach headed for the M4.

"Saw you on telly last night, or rather heard about you on some Cheltenham Festival preamble stuff," said Carter softly, his eyes still closed.

Christine shrugged but sat up attentively and said in a resigned but matter-of-fact manner : "So you know then: I work for *The Times*."

"And what do you campaign for?" asked Carter. "The journalist said that you were a campaigner. Save the Whale or something like that?" There was flippancy in his tone.

Noting the flippancy, Christine replied: "Yes, something like that." Carter waited for her to go on but she didn't. Instead, she looked out of the window pointedly, her lips firmly closed and snubbed Carter with her body language. He pursed his lips, raised his eyebrows and nodded ever so slightly at the snub. It mattered to him—her disapproval—and he didn't know why. She was nobody, he said to himself, she was a mere Earthling, a nothing. But it did matter and the fact frustrated him deeply. Why did he care? Why?

It was on the outskirts of Oxford before she spoke again and, when she did, her voice was calm but strong: "I am a founder member of the campaign organisation called S.O.S, which is dedicated to—"

"Save Our Souls from what we are doing to ourselves," interrupted Carter, chuckling inwardly at the word 'we'. "Very laudable, better now that you have put your bombs away, better by far. Got the ear of the United States, this place, the majority of Europe and even China. But how does *The Times* take it?" Carter noticed the relaxing of her shoulders and slightly animated expression on her face. She was clearly passionate about her subject and it was his too, ironically. They had a lot in common but he couldn't tell her about that… at least, not yet.

"As I am sure you know, we have gone back to being a broadsheet," she began. "We have severed all links with social media and concentrate solely on the printed word. We have, in fact, un-invented the wheel. It was quite a gamble, I can tell you, but it is paying off. And, to answer your question, *The Times* top brass have close ties with S.O.S., very close ties. They 'take it', as you put it, very well." Christine turned and looked at him for the first time. She was triumphant and Carter felt a strange warmth flood his being.

"So why are you going to do a 'colour piece'– that's what you call it, isn't it?—on Cheltenham Festival?"

"My boss doesn't want me to become too obsessed. He wants me to lighten up a bit. I take his point. How about you? What do you do?" The question came quickly, naturally, but Carter was not expecting it and his mind raced.

"I'm in export and import, travel a lot, live out of a suitcase most of the time…" he lied casually, believably.

"Pretty boring actually. Your job sounds much more exciting. Tell me more."

So she did, until they reached Northleach, a few miles from Cheltenham. But more about S.O.S. than about *The Times*, which Carter was pleased about.

"We're nearly there," he broke in.

John Carter was not the only person to hear what Christine had to say. In the back seat, next to a side window, sat a man in his mid-forties, head behind a copy of the *Daily Mail*. In his right ear was an unsuspicious, white earpiece which was tuned into the magnetic, electronic bug the man had stuck underneath Carter's seat, when he knelt down to 'do up' his shoelaces, on his way to ask the driver some spurious question at Victoria Coach Station. The man had heard everything the couple had said and he smiled thinly at what he had heard.

2

The National Express coach pulled into Royal Well Coach Station and disgorged its passengers, John Carter and Christine Jackson walking side by side, rather aimlessly, and a small, middle-aged man striding up the Promenade with a purposeful gait.

"That man…" Christine trailed.

Carter frowned and looked around him. "What man?" he asked.

"He was listening to our every word," she said, "and he wasn't reading his newspaper, he didn't turn a page the whole way, and why is he in such a hurry?" She looked at the back of the small, middle-aged man and narrowed her eyes.

"Come on," said Carter impatiently. "Do you fancy a drink? Maybe here in town or in Pittville. Nice little boozer near where I live. Called the Sudeley Arms."

"Let's go there," she said. She carried her holdall easily with the other hand and he struggled with his two bright red suitcases.

After ten minutes, they were walking up the steps to the Sudeley and, once inside, they ordered their drinks and flopped onto a settee in the lounge bar.

The pub had been taken over and totally refurbished five years ago. From a cheap, dismal boozer, it had been transformed into a rather chic establishment. More expensive but far nicer than it had been before: carpeted throughout, high quality furnishings and furniture, a pleasant restaurant area, two good bars and two beautiful en suite rooms above, to rent on a bed-and-breakfast basis. And customers!

Christine said, twirling her glass of white wine absentmindedly and frowning: "What was that man all about? Why was he listening to us? Why did he walk off in so much of a hurry? Umm…"

Carter returned her frown and replied: "I really don't know but why on earth are you so interested… dare I say it, obsessed… with this man, who seemed pretty ordinary to me?"

Christine looked down at the floor for several seconds before she answered: "Because I think he was watching us, more likely me, and I know this sounds paranoid but I think it is because of my association with S.O.S."

"Then why did he make off in the opposite direction? Why didn't he follow us here?"

"That's what I would like to know… and it worries me. No matter, it's my problem, not yours. Let's talk about racing."

Which they did for two hours and four drinks apiece until Christine turned to face Carter and said, suddenly: "Could you ask the landlord if one of the rooms is free tonight? I would like to stay here. Not at the swanky Queen's Hotel," she pulled a face and then smiled, a shade too quickly.

"But I thought you were booked in there," said Carter. "You *do* know that it's race week and the chance of finding anywhere else to stay is remote, to say the least."

Carter went to the bar and asked the barman if he could

see Tom, the landlord, for a second. He wanted to know if there was a room free. The barman nodded, picked up the phone and, after a couple of minutes, returned to the bar.

"Down in a sec," he said.

Tom O'Flanagan was a big, smiling, beer-bellied Irishman with a huge heart and a small degree of tolerance for trouble-makers. He ran a happy, fun pub but it was a tight ship, where the highest of standards was expected of staff and customers alike. He was responsible for the refurb and it was a majority of his own money that had made it possible. So he guarded his Sudeley Arms with a gentle fierceness. He stormed into the bar and clapped Carter jovially on both arms.

"By some sort of fluke, Johnny, old friend, I had an unexpected cancellation d'is very morning," he said. "D'ere is a room free."

There was a theatrical largesse about the man. You couldn't help smiling, which Carter and Christine found that they were doing. "Let me show you, young lady… I presume it's for you?… just you follow me."

And she did.

Twenty minutes later, Tom and Christine returned to the bar, both smiling, and Christine sat down next to Carter and patted his arm enthusiastically. She drained her wine, rather inelegantly, and announced: "Let's have some more. We've got something to toast now: five nights, bed and breakfast, at the Sudeley Arms. And the room is lovely." She gave a thumbs-up to Tom.

****

Conrad Stone walked officiously into the Queen's Hotel and straight up to the reception desk, suitcase in one hand, umbrella in the other. The small, middle-aged man in a crumpled suit and off-white shirt leant forward to address the youngster sitting down behind the desk.

"My daughter is booked in here," Stone said. "My daughter's name is Christine Jackson. I am Derek Jackson, her father. Has she checked in yet?"

The youngster, who had been just employed from the job centre for a week's temporary work, looked at the register with clear trepidation, running his fingers down a list of names.

"Oh yes, I can see her name now sir. Room 12, on the first floor," said the youngster. "Oh but I'm not supposed to say that," he added and looked up but Stone had already turned his back, picked up his case and walked away towards the main entrance. He had what he came for—her room number.

Stone climbed into a taxi he had pre-booked, whispered the name of the hotel to the driver, and sat back to watch the pavements of racegoers lurching by. He smiled thinly at the havoc he was going to wreak. Their silly bets and boasts, their fake fun, their ridiculous garb and their stupid banter. They would shut up for a while at what he was going to do.

Stone had booked a room at the Holiday Inn for just one night and the first thing that he did when he got there was to phone his contact number. No name, just a contact number, which he was to delete as soon as the phone call was over. He explained the situation and was told to go ahead. He nodded, smiled into the phone, put it down on a table and flopped on to a settee, eyes closed and still smiling. Quarter of a million pounds was a lot of money, he thought, a lot of money!

****

Clean Oil Global was huge. It, as its name suggested, spanned the world with 27 companies dotted all over the globe—Europe, the UK, the United States, the Middle East, Africa, Australia, India, et al.—and it controlled the oil market, which, despite the efforts of S.O.S. and others, including governments, to curtail its might, it was still thriving. Thanks to one thing, one ingredient added to every single litre of the stuff, be it petrol, aviation fuel or whatever. Just one tiny ingredient, which transformed the fossil fuel monster into a green paragon of virtue. And, understandably, the conglomerate protected that ingredient fanatically. It was, after all, their pot of gold at the end of the rainbow.

Clean Oil Global was formed in 2027 and, for five years, had grown and grown… and kept the planes flying and the cars running… and kept open garages selling only its petrol. And, most importantly, it had successfully put up two fingers at many green movements who were suspicious of this 'new ingredient'. Movements like S.O.S.

The new ingredient went by the name of carbonite and was said to eradicate all carbon emissions, rendering fossil fuels harmless to the Earth's atmosphere. It had been rigorously tested and given the go-ahead by governments worldwide. Save Our Souls and a few other pressure groups were not so sure. They saw carbonite as a scam, a worldwide scam. Having carried out tests of their own, they said that they had found the additive to do nothing but eliminate the odour of oil. As for rendering fossil fuels harmless to the Earth's atmosphere they said that this contention was simply not true. Quite understandably, for huge financial reasons, S.O.S. was not too popular with Clean Oil Global. And Christine Jackson was a leading light in the organisation… and wrote for *The Times*. A double whammy!

So, the services of one Conrad Stone were required, for a fee, a huge fee, of course. And Stone had already made his plans: he knew her room number and he was very clear about what he had to do and how he was going to do it. A direct, one-to-one hit was out of the question. It was too obvious and would make his target an overnight sacrificial lamb and would very soon point the finger firmly at Clean Oil. No, that was not on. Christine Jackson had to die alongside some others and he knew a way.

****

The middle-aged man who swaggered into the Queens Hotel that evening was clearly a racegoer: bright pink shirt, cream cravat, tweed jacket, pink trousers, light brown suede shoes and a ticket around his neck swinging from a lanyard. He reached the reception desk (the youngster had gone off shift and had been replaced by a tired and grumpy-looking man) and he leant over to ask if there was a room vacant. The grumpy man shook his head without a word and Conrad Stone replied: "That's a shame, a real shame, because my daughter is staying here and I would dearly like to see her. Has she checked in yet, it's Room 12," he added casually.

The grumpy man looked at the register, running his forefinger down the list of names, looked up and said: "Yes, she must have done. Room is now occupied. They have just arrived."

They? thought Stone with a slightly puzzled frown. He tried a winning smile, turned and swaggered off across the now bustling room.

After half an hour in the cocktail bar, Stone, carrying an overnight bag, caught the lift to the first floor, where he walked past Room 12 and entered the gentlemen's toilet at the end of the corridor. Once inside a cubicle, he opened his holdall, spent quarter of an hour fixing a timer to the incendiary device, returned the primed package, which was wrapped in pink paper, to the holdall, left the cubicle and the toilet and walked back up the corridor, where he stopped at Room 12. He waited for the coast to be clear then he extracted the incendiary device and leant it against the door. 'Have a great race week and enjoy!' was scrawled on a greetings card stuck to the package. He beat a hasty retreat out of the hotel and into a waiting taxi, which he had booked earlier. Ten minutes later, the device went off. Stone was a mile-and-a-half away at the time. He was on his way to the Gupsill Manor Hotel on the outskirts of Tewkesbury.

****

John Carter crossed the road from Pittville Lawn to the Sudeley Arms and walked in, scouting from left to right to see if Christine was already there. And she was, behind a glass of wine. She smiled radiantly and patted the seat next to her. He joined her, feeling an unfamiliar sensation of relief that she was there. He smiled back and tried, unsuccessfully, to wipe away the strange but pleasant sensation. He looked into her eyes, smiled back and sat down. They looked at each other for a long time before he finally spoke.

Ten minutes later, they heard the sirens. Tom turned on the television, Carter and Christine looked up at the screen without a word and twenty minutes later a newsflash commanded the attention of the whole, crowded bar. The presenter was talking excitedly and looking straight at the camera and behind him stood the Queen's Hotel, with half a dozen fire engines and two ambulances parked outside. Smoke billowed from the first floor windows and a crowd had, of course, gathered.

Four rooms on the first floor had been gutted by the fire, but, sadly two people—a man and woman—died from smoke inhalation and burns. Their names were Sophie Johnson and Bernard Johnson. They were in Room 12.

Christine stared at Carter, open-mouthed, reached across the small, round table in front of them and clutched his hand tightly.

"I was booked into Room 12—I didn't tell them that I wasn't going to take the room."

3

This was John Carter's third visit to Earth.

Carter, along with a couple of hundred others, left their own planet and travelled to Planet Earth some 200,000 years ago. The idea was to plant a mind in the species of a superior life force. And see what would happen, see what they would do to their own planet.

The brain—which had already resulted in the descendants of apes standing on just two legs (homo erectus) and using the other two as arms, therefore fashioning crude tools and soon becoming superior to the other animals—only acted on commands and was not able to think, other than to survive. Instinct. But the mind was altogether different. Put the two together and monitor the results.

There was a purpose, a reason. But more of that later…

John Carter and others discovered that homo erectus lived in caves on the African continent, and were hunter/gatherers. These early precursors of Modern Man were going around in circles, not getting anywhere and never going to rise above what, after all, they were—only sophisticated animals. Unless they had minds… to adapt, improve, advance, progress. To tell the brain what to do, not just to rely on instinct to merely survive. To think.

And so Carter and his men travelled across every continent of the planet, but concentrating on Africa as this was the hotbed of homo sapiens. They planted the thought process along the way, which would spread only among Modern Man and would not affect any other animal. It would spread in much the way a viral pandemic spreads, but even more virulently. Job done they returned to their own planet, which was dying because of them and shared their experiences. A meeting of the minds, so to speak. They waited…

****

Christine Jackson had been up most of the night, talking to her editor, the police and filing copy to *The Times*. She had told the police that she had been booked into Room 12 but had decided to stay elsewhere and had failed to inform the hotel. She told Sir Jeremy Butcher, the editor of *The Times* (who was mightily relieved that his star reporter was still alive), the whole story and her beat on it, especially about the middle-aged man who seemed to have a suspect interest in her, and then she filed her copy. It made the front page on the following day. WAS S.O.S. ACTIVIST THE TARGET? ran the banner headline and below was a picture of Christine and her by-lined story.

She did not mention John Carter, much to his relief, when he bought a copy of the newspaper from the local shop at 9.00am. He looked long and hard at her photograph. Her eyes were soft and tender and Carter touched the picture gently. Closing his own eyes and shrugging almost angrily, he tried to rid himself of the totally irrational feelings that he had. He did not realise that his mind and hers had already formed an attachment. Such things were alien to him; he did not understand them.

Carter telephoned Christine and heard a sleepy voice ask what time was it. Not 'who was it?' because she knew it was him and it was only from a feeling that she had.

"It is half-past midday, do you fancy a drink?" he said, a pause and then, "I'll be in the pub in about half an hour … if I can get through the inevitable crowds."

She nodded into the phone and then switched it off. She swung out of bed, standing up and running her fingers through her hair, looked at her naked body in a mirror and suddenly felt huge relief that she was still alive. She had a shower, dressed and went downstairs, into the bar, which was, as per Carter's words, full of "the inevitable crowds".

But she saw Tom—tall and huge—rising up above the others in the middle of the room. Tom bent his head to one of the men at a round table and all four got to their feet promptly. Tom beckoned for Christine to take a seat and, with relief, she did. It was a chaotic pub and after all it had been a long night.

"Is he coming in?" Tom asked, swigging at a pint of Guinness, wiping the froth away from his lips with the back of his hand and plonking the glass down on to the table. Not his name, just 'he'.

Christine nodded and so did the landlord, before wandering off into the midst of the crowds, clapping one or two on the backs in friendly recognition.

Carter threaded his way through the throng and sat down beside Christine. He was carrying a folded copy of *The Times*, which he laid out on the table between them.

"Good piece," he said. "So you're off to Birmingham for the COP conference? What capacity are you going—reporter or activist?"

Christine raised her eyebrows and shrugged: "My editor thinks that I am just going to report on the thing. But I shall be putting on my S.O.S. hat from time to time," she said with a cheeky smile, her hand up to her mouth. Carter also raised his eyebrows. That smile, that smile… he thought.

"How long is the conference?" asked Carter.

"It's for five days at the National Exhibition Centre in Solihull and starts next Monday. I'm going to be busy. But until then…" she trailed, picking up her glass of wine and raising it to the bar-room in general.

****

"That roar of the crowd when the first race started…" she said, shaking her head against the pillow and closing her eyes delightedly. He was lying on his back and staring up at the ceiling. He didn't know what was happening and why, but all that he did know was that he had never felt so happy. Carter turned his head, leant across and kissed her on her left temple. She squirmed with pleasure and snuggled down in the bed. Carter put his arm around her and looked again up at the ceiling. How much should he tell her? He asked himself the question. How much?

"Do you want to talk?" he asked and she nodded, rearranging herself to lie on her back next to him. There was a long delay before he spoke again, maybe five minutes or so.

"I am not from here," he said softly. "I am from another planet… and this is not my body."

"Seemed all right to me," she broke in coquettishly. He ignored her.

"This is my third visit here—the first was a long time, a very long time ago and the second was about 2,000 years ago—and now this."

"Go on," she said quietly, the journalist in her waking up suddenly, eyes wide open with concentration. She knew that he was telling the truth. She also knew that Sir Jeremy Butcher would never hear of this conversation and neither would anybody else. And Carter knew that too.

"My planet is on the other side of the universe, and we will live forever," he began, still staring up at the ceiling. "We do not have bodies now, only minds. We have evolved as far as we can. Minds that last forever. We can never change, never go back now to what we were… and that is sad, so very sad."

There was a long pause before Christine said: "But you have a body—we have just made love—so what is this all about?"

Carter shrugged, closed his eyes and shook his head: "I don't know, I really don't know. Something has happened to me, something that I don't understand. And it is all to do with… you."

Christine shot Carter a curious look, a frown almost, and said: "What have I got to do with this?"

"I don't know, I don't know…" he said, an element of despair in his voice. "I'm sorry but I don't know what you have done to me."

Christine nestled into Carter's right shoulder but spoke firmly, in control now: "Love. That is the word. We have fallen in love. And there can be no explanation, there never is, but that is what has happened, that is what I have done to you… and what you have done to me. Love.”

Carter was silent for a long time before he said, in a quiet voice: “What *is* love? I have heard of it of course but I have never experienced it, never. I have got a mind and at the moment I have a body and a brain which my people created, but where does love come into it?”

Christine shrugged a little helplessly. “I’ve been in love once before and I love you now.”

Carter gazed at her for a very long time. “And I think that I must… love… you. Bloody hell,” he added and immediately apologised for the mild profanity.

Christine merely shook her head and grinned. “Go on…” she said. “Carry on with your story.”

“I am here now to find out how close you are, the human race is, to extinction. Climate change, in short. The polar ice is melting, your rivers are heavily polluted, the fossil fuel emissions are playing havoc with the Earth’s atmosphere, you are destroying the very air that you breathe, your weather is becoming more severe, there are wildfires that rip through your towns, you are killing yourselves and every other living creature there is… like we did to our own planet, many, many years ago.”

“You say that I am doing this!” exclaimed Christine with quiet anger. “I am not. What about S.O S?”

“No, no, no, not you,” corrected Carter, squeezing her gently. “But you know what I mean. This planet is on borrowed time. A matter of a few years, if that. And it is all because of greed, avarice, a constant hunger for more and more… at any cost. And the cost is huge—numerous species are dying out all the time, the land and sea are changing, more extremes of temperature are causing widespread fires and floods and all because of Man's greed."

"So what are you going to do about it?" Christine asked.

"I don't know yet," replied Carter. "That's enough for now." He turned his back and she spooned him.

4

The train from Cheltenham Spa to Birmingham New Street was six carriages long. It was on time and was less than half full. So Carter and Christine had no difficulty finding a table seat. It was good to be leaving Cheltenham after the madness of race week. It had been quite a few days. They both felt a sense of enormous relief.

They had quit the town and were coasting through the green and lush Vale of Evesham when Carter was first to break the silence.

"Have you ever read Erich von Daniken?" he asked.

"*Chariot of the Gods, Was God an Astronaut?* is his most famous book," Christine replied like a shot. "It was published in 1968 but he has since written many other books. Similar subject matter. Do you know that he sold more than 60 million copies of his books?"

Carter was impressed and he raised his eyebrows in appreciation and gave her a long look, nodding his head. "Yes, in short he believed—and he backed this up with historical conundrums—that alien beings from another planet visited Earth many thousands of years ago.

"They even found cave drawings of what appeared to be men in space suits in South America and elsewhere. He was convinced that Earth had been visited on several occasions by these aliens, for want of a better word. Does any of this interest you?"

Christine looked out of the window. "Oh yes, it does, it really does. I am convinced that they—whoever they are—came here but what I don't know is why they came..." she trailed, shaking her head. Suddenly, she leant over the table, put her fingers under Carter's chin, lifted it up until he was looking at her and added: "Unless you know, of course."

Carter smiled. "I do... of course. But don't you think that I am some lune, that I should be locked up? Why on earth do you believe me, why?"

"Because," she replied with a shrug, looking back over the English countryside—a green land that would soon be brown, she thought grimly—passing by without a murmur. "Because I do believe you, just because," she added lamely but honestly. "But I still don't know why, I don't know why you are here... now."

"I will tell you soon," he said gently, looking her straight in the eyes, "I will tell you soon."

She leant over the table and kissed him tenderly on the cheek. "Okay," she said and summoned a woman pushing a trolley down the aisle. She ordered two beers.

Unbeknownst to Carter and Christine, Conrad Stone was just two carriages behind them. You would not recognise him. The small, middle-aged, somewhat scruffy man now wore a neatly-trimmed, but full, black beard, a pair of horn-rimmed glasses, a black hat and he was dressed in a smart, dark grey suit, with a white shirt and plain, blue tie. His shoes were black and shiny. There was a brown suede briefcase on the seat next to him. Stone was concentrating on his mobile phone, hands flying over the keys as he sent some message. He appeared to be the consummate businessmen.

****

Sir Jeremy Butcher put down the telephone carefully, pulled a face and stared at the portrait of Winston Churchill on the wall opposite him. He was not a happy man. It had been a difficult telephone call, to put it mildly. What would the great man have done, he thought, still looking into the eyes of Churchill and chewing his lower lip?

The call had been from the chairman of *The Times* board of directors—the main man. And it was clear that his bosses (and the people who held the purse strings) were not happy about Christine Jackson's association with S.O.S. They wanted her to choose: the activist group or the newspaper. One or the other. Simple as that.

Sir Jeremy knew what she would say. She would resign her job from *The Times* in a flash and commit all her time to the S.O.S. And he would have lost his best writer just like that. What was he to do? Winston offered no help and so he looked away.

After about ten minutes, with a huge sigh, he reached for the telephone and dialled Christine's mobile number.

****

Conrad Stone checked into a pleasant, four-star hotel close to the railway station and registered as John Rawlings. He took his holdall up to his third-floor room, lay it on the bed and examined the contents. The contents included an alarm clock, a length of wire, a fuse and a bomb. There was enough plastic explosive to cause significant damage to a large roomful of people.

He took off his glasses, beard wig and tie and flopped onto the bed, still smarting from the ticking off he had received from his contact in Clean Oil Global. But he was £50,000 to the better so he didn't feel too bad about it. He closed his eyes and thought about the £200,000 he was going to receive for causing the disruption intended to firmly point the finger at the Save Our Souls action group. That villa in Spain sounded pretty good.

****

Clean Oil Global had their UK head office in Tilbury on the eastern side of London. It was a former warehouse complex for the docks, converted by Clean Oil Global into pleasant and efficient offices. One department was accessed by a single door, always manned by two security guards. On the door was a plaque which read 'Security department: no admittance'. Inside was an open-plan office with 22 desks, sporting lap-tops and telephones, and at the back were four private offices, the one on the far right bearing a plaque which read 'Department Head'.

The department head replaced the receiver on the handset, turned in the swivel chair behind his desk to look out of the window at the grey waters of the Thames estuary and smiled enigmatically. He closed his eyes briefly and nodded his head, although he was alone in the office. He reached for the telephone on his desk.

"Is that you, Conrad?" he asked, and a muffled voice said yes.

****

"I have resigned from *The Times*," said Christine flatly and then sipped at her glass of wine. They were at a bar in Solihull. "Sir Jeremy gave me two choices—the paper or my association with S.O.S. He said my activism was not good for my health—what he really meant was that it was not good for *The Times*. So I made my choice and resigned. So I am now a full-time activist but unemployed."

Carter pursed his lips, shrugged and said: "Was that a good idea? What about the conference?"

"Oh, I have agreed to continue to cover COP32 but after that I am leaving," Christine said. "I shall be a lady of leisure," she added with a smile. Carter smiled too.

"I shall be on the press bench for one last time," she went on. "And you, my friend, have got a ticket for the first event. It's Clean Oil Global, making a presentation on what wonderful work they do. I should co-co. But I will keep my lips sealed and you can make your own mind up. They say that carbonite—their *special* ingredient—makes oil, and therefore petrol, diesel and aviation fuel—safe to use without harming the environment. They say that carbonite renders their oil completely harmless. And they say that they have scientists and governments to support their case. But, as I've said before, it's a load of crap. Carbonite only eradicates the odour of oil and the fossil fuel does as much damage as it did before. But they have, globally, trillions of pounds to support their contention. They even have scientific and governmental so-called evidence to back up what they say."

Carter challenged her: "How do you know that it's a load of crap, as you call it? How do you know that carbonite does not do what they say it does? How do you argue with scientists and with governments? Surely you are pretty much of a loser."

"John…" Christine began sternly, "this is the whole point. It's all about money. And S.O.S. has employed its own scientists to examine carbonite and the effect it has on oil. The conclusions are simple: it is, as I've said before (she managed a rather coy smile), a load of crap. Carbonite does nothing, absolutely nothing, to prevent petrol, diesel and aviation fuel from destroying our atmosphere and ultimately us.

"But Clean Oil Global makes billions of pounds and dollars every hour on selling the stuff to airlines, garages and to governments worldwide. They put money and profit above the survival of our planet. And they have enough of that to buy off governments, yes governments."

Christine was breathless with excitement—this was obviously her pet subject—and she lowered her outstretched hands to mark a calming down. Carter smiled and held one of her hands affectionately.

"You feel strongly about this, don't you," he spoke quietly. And she nodded like a little girl. "And you are covering this presentation," he added conversationally. "And take care, please take care. I have a funny feeling about tomorrow."

****

The middle-aged man in a light blue boiler suit with the Clean Oil Global logo on the back drew little attention from the N.E.C. security guys who had done their job for the day and were getting ready to go home. The Clean Oil Global logo was the Planet Earth held in a cupped hand with the name of the consortium top and bottom. It was very eye-catching. The man was squeezing up the aisles between the seats placing leaflets on each one. He had 250 seats to do. His holdall was by a corner in the wall, near the fixed fire extinguisher, bulging with leaflets. In the bottom of the bag were the plastic explosive, alarm clock and fuse.

He showed his ID and introduced himself as a certain John Rawlings. After a quick security check with Clean Oil Global in East London, the Birmingham security men were satisfied. They told Rawlings to tell reception when he was finished and they left him to it.

Conrad Stone (alias John Rawlings) made his way along an aisle and came to the corner where the fire extinguisher was placed, on the ground and, much to his relief, free-standing. Not checking that the coast was clear—he knew that CCTV was in action—Stone, with his back to the camera, put the bomb, clock and fuse quickly behind the fire extinguisher and continued, for several minutes, to fiddle with the bright red contraption, as if he was making sure that it was secure. He then continued to leaflet the seating. For around half an hour. He then left the room, holding his holdall casually, checked out at reception and took a taxi back to his hotel. He was not followed.

He changed his clothing and went back down to the bar, where he ordered a small whisky and water and settled back in an armchair near a window. The small smile on his face was barely noticeable. *£200,000, done and almost dusted*, he thought with mild satisfaction. He texted head of security at Clean Oil Global with a simple message: 'Sorted.' The head of security nodded at his mobile phone screen and deleted the message, without replying.

Conrad Stone decided to have another whisky, this time a large one, and he sat back down in the armchair, squirming with pleasure. It had been a good day's work. And a profitable one.

****

"So why did you come here again and why now?" Christine asked after her third large glass of wine.

Carter made a helpless gesture with his arms and shook his head. He closed his eyes for a few seconds before answering.

"I said that I would tell you one day," he began and then looked her in the eyes and gazed down at the floor for a long time. "But I suppose that one day is here. I suppose that I will have to tell you now. But can we go over there and sit down. The barman seems very interested in what we are talking about and I'd rather not say what I am going to say within his earshot."

They carried their drinks over and sat down in the corner of the room, much to the barman's disappointment. He had been listening to every word.

"To put it simply, I am here again to evaluate the situation. In other words, has the experiment worked, has Man become more caring, more humane, more concerned about this planet? That is why I am here, Christine (he used her name for the first time). Has the union of the brain and mind created a more compassionate being? Or has the combination just resulted in greed, at the expense of all others?"

"And what about us?" asked Christine in a soft voice.

Carter froze and looked out of the window. Why did that question mean so much to him? What was it all about? What was happening… to him? He tussled in his fine mind but could not come up with the answer.

"I don't know, I really don't know," he said lamely.

And Christine leant across and touched his hand tenderly. He gripped hard, closed his eyes, took a deep breath and continued, in a measured fashion.

"Us?" Carter spoke brokenly. "What does that mean, what the hell does that mean?" He paused before continuing in a calmer tone, "All I know is that I have inexplicable feelings for you… and I also know that you feel the same about me. But I don't know why.

"Love is a strange word, a strange concept, to say the least, but it needs examination. Because it is a real emotion, an emotion that I do not understand, an emotion that my planet does not understand. But an emotion, that, for some reason, millions of others have. But what is it?"

Christine thought for a while and then replied: "Love is love, as simple as that. You cannot rationalise it, you cannot even explain it… Maybe it's the result of a combination of the mind and the brain. The spirit, the soul."

Carter nodded and gave her hand a lingering pat. "Maybe the mind and brain are just not enough. Maybe the spirit and the soul are necessary… whatever they are."

"So what is your conclusion to all this?" she asked. "Are we worth saving?"

"*You* are," Carter grinned, "but I can't speak for all the other millions."

"Let's lighten up." She picked up both glasses and got to her feet.

5

The bomb went off at 11.35 in the morning of the following day. It sent splinters of glass and wood flying in all directions. There was a lot of smoke and a fire had broken out. Seeing that the device was positioned behind the fire extinguisher, the people had to wait for the fire brigade to tackle the blaze.

Two—both employed by Clean Oil Global in middle management positions—died in the explosion. Four people—also employees of Clean Oil Global—were severely injured and 12 others received minor injuries.

The press bench, which included four photographers and a BBC film cameraman, besides Christine Jackson, was on the opposite side of the room, below several tiers of members of the public, which included John Carter.

It was, of course, mayhem, unmitigated mayhem, but the photographers on the press bench had a field day, especially the man from the Beeb.

Christine dialled the private number of Sir Jeremy, got through almost immediately and told him what had happened. She then rattled off some holding copy and said that she would phone back in 30 minutes with a more substantial story. This was one time Sir Jeremy regretted having severed all links with social media. And so, Christine got to work. In 45 minutes, she filed her story and it had it all: how many casualties, what the response factor (fire, police, ambulance) was, what damage had been caused and statements from Clean Oil Global and the chief executive of the National Exhibition Centre. She had put on her reporter's hat instinctively and there was no question of her voicing her own views, which were mixed, to say the least.

She then found Carter, slightly bemused by the whole business and standing outside the centre with a bewildered look on his face. She fell into his arms and started to sob, at the sheer horror of what had happened but also with relief that he was all right.

They watched the BBC news bulletin two hours later in the bar of their hotel, along with a goodly number of others, who all looked anxious and horrified at the same time.

After outlining the facts, the presenter added: "The blame is being placed at the doorstep of the Save Our Planet action group and the police are now investigating their possible involvement. We shall bring you further reports as soon as we can…"

Carter swivelled and looked into Christine's eyes, but he did not say a word. Christine simply shook her head and Carter nodded.

****

Sir Jeremy Butcher ushered Christine into his office, indicated a chair in front of his desk for her to sit down, walked around the mahogany beast and arranged himself in a dark green, leather swivel chair. He rested his chin on his hands on the desk and looked long and hard at his number one writer, or was she his ex-number one writer? She returned his gaze.

"Christ, I'm glad you are all right, I am really glad," he said quietly. "And now to business. I supposed you wondered why I asked you to come in. Well, it is simple really." He leant back in his chair, staring up at the ceiling, before looking at her again. "I want you to retract your notice, I want you to stay on."

"But I am not going to quit S.O.S. I thought that was clear, I thought that you knew that," she said with a puzzled frown on her face. "I thought you said that I had to choose, one or the other."

"I have changed my mind," Sir Jeremy said with a sigh. "I don't want to lose you."

Christine got up, walked around the desk and kissed Sir Jeremy on the cheek. She then returned to her chair. Her editor put his fingers up to his cheek where she had kissed him, fought back the tears that threatened to force their way out and smiled.

"You are going to be in trouble now," she said and he nodded.

****

The police investigated and Christine was among those questioned, of course, although her presence at the Clean Oil Global presentation not only gave her a solid alibi but it also meant that she or her organisation could not possibly have been so involved. It would have been suicidal. It however did not stop the press from having a bean feast and it did not stop Clean Oil Global from shedding crocodile tears over the casualties, taking opportunities for strongly hinting at S.O. S.

being the culprits and that carbonite was everything they said it was.

DID S.O.S. PLANT THE BOMB? Ran the front-page banner headline in *The Sun*. WERE ACTIVISTS RESPONSIBLE? asked *The Daily Mirror*. CLEAN OIL GLOBAL SAY THEY ARE ONLY TRYING TO HELP THE PLANET suggested *The Guardian*. And so on and so forth. But, as Christine told Carter philosophically in the Sudeley Arms over a drink or two later in the week: "Today's shit hot topic… but tomorrow's chip paper." She had to explain the journalistic simile to Carter who nodded in agreement.

"When are you planning to go back to London?" he asked.

"Don't know exactly. Can I stay with you for a few days?"

"Of course you can," he replied quickly. She noted his eagerness and raised her eyebrows. He merely grinned… a shade lasciviously.

They went for a walk in nearby Pittville Park and sat down on a park bench overlooking the upper lake. It was quiet and peaceful and, apart from two swans and their six signets and a handful of ducks, they were alone. A middle-aged Asian man walked along the lake on the opposite side. He looked to be in a hurry. Christine froze and her eyes widened. She craned forwards and stared at the man, who was some 50 metres away on the other side of the lake and almost scuttling along a path towards a set of bushes. Above stood Pittville Pump Rooms, proud and austere, at the head of a downward slope of green, green grass.

Christine stood up frantically, reached for her mobile phone in the back pocket of her jeans and took several photographs of the man before he disappeared behind the bushes. She then plonked herself down again on the bench beside Carter, who was looking at her with a puzzled frown on his face.

"What was that all about?" he asked.

"It's that man… the man on the coach here…the man who was listening to our every word," she spoke urgently and was breathing hard.

Carter was concerned, but he was also sceptical. "Calm down, Christine, please calm down. And, in any event, the man on the coach was not an Asian, he was not wearing a sari and a turban and he did not have a full black beard. So it is not the same man. What makes you think that it is?"

"It's the way he walks," said Christine softly. "You can dye your skin, wear whatever clothing you wish, put on a fake beard, use any disguise you like… but you cannot disguise the way that you walk, especially if your mind is elsewhere. He walks just the same as our man, with a sort of hasty shuffle, a quickstep, a forward-leaning gait. I noticed it when he left the coach to hurry up the Prom on the day of the hotel fire."

She paused and put a finger to her lips: "In fact, I have always had a vague idea that he had something to do with that fire. Don't know what… but I have always suspected it."

"Do you want to report it to the police?"

Christine shook her head and smiled cynically. Carter knew what she meant and he didn't add anything.

"Just keep an eye out for him… in the Sudeley… he might go there," she said. And Carter nodded.

"Let's go and have a coffee," he said and she got up with a grin.

****

Conrad Stone had seen Christine jump to her feet and take photographs of him; he immediately realised she knew that it was him.

He decided that he would not act any further against her, without specific orders to do so from the head of security at Clean Oil Global. Instead, he would concentrate on his next task, which he was looking forward to. There was plenty of time for Christine Jackson.

****

Christine Jackson was 34 years old. She was an adopted child—her mother and father had both been killed in a car accident—and she was sent to a boarding school, exclusively for girls, at the age of eleven. She was a bright child and English was always her favourite subject, at which she excelled. Her teacher (and mentor) was the Head of English at her House and he took her under his wing. He knew that she had a special ability at writing and he nurtured it well. She excelled at the subject and later went to Oxford University to get her 1st class degree, with honours!

Afterwards, she went travelling for the best part of a year and then, at the age of 22, flew through a diploma in a journalism course and got a job as a reporter on a small weekly in the Midlands, *The Gloucester Express*. She was then given a job by the BBC as a reporter and after two years became one of the main news presenters. She was just 26 when the editor of *The Times* saw one of her broadcasts. Mightily impressed, Sir Jeremy Butcher wanted to meet her and discuss a possible future with his newspaper.

When they met, it took Sir Jeremy less than two minutes to come to a decision that he wanted her on his staff. It took Christine about the same amount of time to decide that she wanted a job on his newspaper, so long as he was the editor.

But always in the background was Christine's passion for the environment and for the reversal of climate change. It helped her through a bad and messy breakup of the first love of her life. A relationship with a married man 20 years her senior, which ended after six months when he went back to his wife. Leaving her lost and unloved.

She was drinking wine with friends of a like mind—two men and two women—in the beer garden of the Prospect of Whitby public house in Wapping. The pub gave out on a sloping green lawn ending at the banks of the river Thames, which was low in water.

"We all agree that we are, as a planet, heading for disaster if we carry on this way," she said and the other three all nodded. "Then why don't we do something about it? Never mind your Smart meters and so on. Why don't we form an action group and try to change the way society thinks?"

The others craned forwards on the table between them and waited for her to continue. Which she did.

And so, Save Our Souls was formed.

And then, of course, Christine Jackson met John Carter…

Carter materialised on Planet Earth and spent more than two years jetting across the world to see and hear firsthand what was happening to the planet. And he was not impressed. His early conclusions were that Earth was heading for self-destruction, that Man appeared to be bent on suicide, that the end of civilisation was just around the corner. And, apart from tokenistic crap, Man was going to do nothing about it.

Because a trait, unknown to Carter, called Greed, had taken centre stage. The experiment was not working or was it working the way it should, was it proving that the mind and brain when together only ever equalled failure? And Carter did not know what to do, especially now. Because now, he had fallen hopelessly in love with Christine Jackson. Whatever love might be.

****

They were lying in bed together, on top of the duvet, both completely naked and side by side. They had just made love and the perspiration gleamed on Carter's forehead and Christine's breasts. They were breathing heavily and their lips were slightly parted. A cool April sun peeped through the curtains and the world was at peace.

"What about the future… what about us?" she asked in a soft voice, staring up at the ceiling.

There was a long pause before Carter spoke, "All I do know is that I am beginning to like this body I have got." He turned and looked at her with a small smile on his face.

She giggled: "So do I. Don't go and exchange it for some old fogey's. I don't do wrinkles very well."

6

They went through the motions for the next few days—eating, sleeping, a couple of drinks at the Sudeley, making love—but they both knew that something had to be said. It was all about the second visit. And Carter had decided to tell her and she knew that.

They sat alone in the pub at a small, round table, a couple of glasses of Merlot in front of them, at around two o'clock one afternoon. There was a tense silence between them and Carter realised that this was the time.

"Do you want to know about my last visit here?" he asked woodenly and Christine closed her eyes and nodded. "My second visit?"

They both reached for their glasses of wine, took deep gulps and leant forward, elbows on the table. Tom, who had been leaning on the bar chatting to them, sensed their need for privacy and he turned and walked away.

"Do you believe in Jesus Christ and all that sort of stuff?" he asked and she shook her head, quite decisively. "Christianity and all that?" And Christine shrugged her shoulders.

"Around 2,000 years ago, the Roman empire was fully in charge of the known world," Carter began. "The Han Dynasty was prevalent in China but in all the Mediterranean land masses the Romans were in complete control. And they were barbaric and cruel. They ruled with a fist of iron and did not suffer fools. They either had them crucified or thrown to the lions. And internally they were completely corrupt. And mad. Emperor Caligula even appointed a horse to his Senate and slept with his own sister. A common thing was incest, among the Roman elite, in those days.

"The Romans had become completely corrupt… and brutal. Power, and they had plenty of that, had taken over their brains. And their minds—minds that we had planted all those years previously—were now filled with debauchery and selfishness. Self-gratification now ruled the roost, as had greed for might. The way they were going, the way in which they were acting, the way in which they were behaving, the way in which they were was conducive to only one thing— the end of civilisation. Suicide."

"So, you had to act," said Christine, who was now alert and expectant and glued to Carter's dialogue. She leant forward and covered his hand with hers. "Go on…"

"Now comes the tricky bit," he said with a faint smile, looking Christine straight in the eye. She waited.

"The initial experiment was to see what happened to mankind if each individual had a mind as well as a brain. Compassion and love were supposed to lead the way. It partially worked, but this attitude of the Romans became the problem. We had to change the way they were going in order to give the experiment time to work. We had to change the mindset."

"But an experiment is just that isn't it… an experiment? The outcome is irrelevant… surely? And if you interfere, aren't you messing around with the experiment itself?"

Christine was emphatic and Carter knew that he had to explain. She was no fool, she asked the right questions.

Carter heaved a very big sigh, closed his eyes briefly, waited for a moment to marshal his thoughts and then continued, "You are right, Christine, of course, you are right. But we had envisaged a different outcome. We did not think that mankind would go the way it did. We were wrong. Openly admit that. And so we changed the rules…" Carter gave an apologetic gesture with his hands and went on: "We had to think how mankind could utilise the gift of a mind, how mankind could avoid extinction. And, believe you me, that was where mankind was headed… extinction. So we introduced love and compassion, instead of hatred and cruelty."

"How?" asked Christine, taking a sip of her wine.

"Religion… or more like Christianity."

Christine closed her eyes and shook her head: "Oh no, not that one? You're going to tell me that you were Jesus Christ or God or something like that. Sorry John, but that would be stretching my powers of belief too far. For God's sake… excuse the pun."

Carter smiled, raised his eyebrows, leant back in his chair, brushed his hair back with a flick of his right hand and then leant forward, across the table between them, inches from her face and said: "I was sent—or rather, my mind was—here with the task of replacing greed, power, cruelty with love and compassion. The experiment was slightly altered to include a belief which we hoped would spread throughout the world. This belief was embodied in an apparently mortal man who would be listened to, followed and copied. He would preach an alternative to violence. Thereby we would save the world from inevitable self-destruction."

"Jesus Christ—the so-called son of God," interjected Christine with mock solemnity. And Carter cocked an eyebrow.

"No, no, not the son of God," he said, shaking his head. "Purely and simply a mind which would invade a host body, who would go among the people and start a quiet but mighty revolution which would change the world. From decadent barbarity to decency. The human race was in great danger. We had to act."

Christine broke in: "But millions of Christians were killed in the Middle Ages by each other: Catholics and Protestants. These uncomfortable bedfellows murdered more, far more, of their own kind than did the Romans. How do you reconcile that?"

Carter said: "In 200AD, Emperor Constantine was converted to Christianity. That spelled the end of the Roman empire. And yes, there was terrible fighting within the realms of Christianity for a long, long time. But our target was the end of the Roman empire and we succeeded in that.

"We had to sit and watch awful butchery in the name of a God whose message was love and compassion. But the overall and penetrating truth was just that: love and compassion. We held our nerve and the killing finally eased."

Christine was, of course, mesmerised. Because she knew that firstly he was not mad and secondly that he was telling the truth. She just knew. She fell silent, willing him to continue.

"The so-called Greatest Story Ever Told is quite simple really," Carter began, draining his wine and indicating to

Tom, who was not far away, for two more glasses. "My mind found a host body—the body of a newly born child—and I bided my time. The baby grew up and became a man. And the man began to preach what was later called the Gospel, the evangelical religion that was to sweep the world.

"Jesus was regarded by the Romans and by the Jewish people to be a threat—he was deemed to be a troublemaker and a terrorist and a vast majority of the inhabitants of Jerusalem and of Israel as a whole wanted him out of the way. But not—and it's a big not—not all. After the crucifixion, some like Paul of Tarsus, thought that the ideology that Jesus preached was worthy of being spread worldwide. Which happened and a different mindset came into being: compassion and love, turning the other cheek instead of hitting back. Christianity."

"With a very small 'c'," whispered Christine.

"Yes, you are right. With a very small 'c'. Never mind all the bullshit divinity which surrounds Christianity," said Carter. "What matters—and it is *all* that matters—is the message of love and compassion. Swinging incense, singing hymns, saying prayers with clasped hands, all that nonsense, is of no value. But the message is *all* that matters."

"So what has gone wrong—why are you back here?" she asked.

"Where do I start?" he asked rhetorically, rocked his head back, eyes closed and thought furiously. She held his hand across the table and he clutched at it until his knuckles were white.

"The human race is heading for destruction in a different way," he began. "Progress is the driving force. You all know, to some degree, that you are heading for extinction. You all know that you are destroying your planet. But you keep on doing it. It is not war, it is not that. It is the unstoppable urge to progress, to have more, to have more. Better and bigger cars, bigger and better houses in which to live. Despite the global political language, the tokenistic verbal garbage, the words, the crap, despite all of that, the truth is very different. You are committing conscious long-term suicide, all for the short-term gain. Greed and that all-important progress are the only forces you care about. But that will destroy you in the end. It is already, it is only a matter of time."

Christine stared long and hard at Carter's despairing face and she slowly shook her head. She loved this man, this mind, or whatever, and she agreed with what he had to say.

"What are we going to do?" she asked and she really meant the question. Carter just looked out of the window. He didn't reply.

There was a long pause before Carter spoke again, "One of your prime ministers—John Major—coined the phrase 'back to basics' some years ago and it is even more appropriate now than it was then," he said. "You must all get back to basics, uninvent the wheel, so to speak, stop this obsession with so-called progress, which is in fact the opposite. Regression. Progress is ensuring that life goes on, regress is what you are doing, ensuring that one day all life on Planet Earth will cease. This must stop and there is no time to lose." Carter spoke with a trace of desperation and Christine picked up on the tone.

"Climate change," she said.

"The most wonderful euphemism in the English language," chuckled Carter. "It used to be called 'global warming' but the powers-that-be reckoned that was too scary and so the phrase 'climate change' was introduced."

"How do we go about uninventing the wheel?" Christine asked. "How the hell do we do that? We must progress—despite what you say about the word, John—we must try to discover a better life. A life of no starvation, no disease, no child mortality. That sort of thing. Surely?"

"Yes of course you are right," said Carter. "But not at the expense of your planet, your very survival. You are up against your biggest and worst enemy—yourselves. That is where the trouble lies."

"So what do we do, what *can* we do?"

"You and S.O.S. are doing great," said Carter reassuringly. "Just carry on with what you are doing—protest and question, always question. It is no good what governments worldwide are doing now. They are only paying lip service to the protesters, they are in the pay of 'progress', they are saying all the right things but not actually doing anything."

"Clean Oil Global," said Christine simply but forcefully. "Clean Oil Global."

Carter nodded, took a sip of wine and carried on: "Yes, if they were gone, if carbonite was discredited as it should be, then a start, a very good start, could be made. But with their billions, their power, that is going to be difficult. Unless somehow the fact that oil, whatever is claimed about carbonite, is not clean and that it is just as bad as any other fossil fuel could be publicised for the whole world to see. Then, with Clean Oil Global out of the way, a new beginning could be in sight."

"I know someone who used to work for them but was given the boot," chipped in Tom, from behind the bar. He had been polishing glasses but he could not help but eavesdrop on some of their conversation. They had been talking quietly but he had very good hearing and, after all, it was a small room. And, after all, what they were talking about was fascinating… and important. The survival of the planet, of mankind. "Do you want to meet him?"

7

Frank Holroyd got a job in the security department of Clean Oil Global six months after he retired from the police force. He had reached the rank of detective inspector and had been based at Gloucester, in the Cotswolds, where he lived with his wife and two children.

Frank rented a bedsit near the Clean Oil Global headquarters in Tilbury, East London, where he stayed during the week, going home to his family for weekends. It was not an ideal situation but the money was good. And his track record as a detective inspector was also good, so he soon got to do more than just routine security jobs.

But being a nosy bloke (it stood him in good stead in the police force), he also found himself listening, or rather eavesdropping, to what was being said by the rather anonymous men at the top. He very soon became suspicious, even more so when he saw Conrad Stone breeze into the office one morning. Fortunately, Frank was in uniform and he pulled his peaked cap firmly over his face. Stone did not recognise him.

Stone went straight to the door of the department head, knocked three times, waited and, as soon as the door was opened, walked in. He was there for a good hour before he emerged, clutching a green file, and left the room, without looking left or right or speaking to anybody.

Frank had arrested Stone a few years ago in connection with a murder inquiry. Stone was known to the police as a suspected contract killer but no evidence had ever been found to support this belief. And yet, Detective Inspector Holroyd had reason to believe (strong gossip on the street) that Stone had been responsible for the death of a middle-aged man. The man, who was blackmailing a top politician at the time, had been shot in the back of the head. But after extensive questioning to no avail, Frank had to let Stone go, without charge.

Frank had seen Stone go into the inner sanctum of Clean Oil Global and that fuelled his desire to know what was going on. It was already clear to him that Clean Oil Global were not so squeaky clean after all, especially if they had associations with the likes of Conrad Stone. And so he set about some serious snooping.

Frank lasted for seven months before he was summoned into the office of the head of security and given his cards. He was told that the department "was cutting back on staff" and he was given a generous redundancy payment, considering how short his tenure had been. He was glad to be leaving and masked his inner grin of satisfaction with a polite nod and a word or two about "I quite understand" and "these are difficult times." With a cheque for £5,000 firmly in his wallet, Frank left the Tilbury building without a backward glance. He found the nearest public house and ordered the first of three large whiskies.

"Keep an eye on Clean Oil Global—I think that all is not right," he told the Metropolitan Police later.

"We already are," was the reply.

Frank, whose family were delighted with what had happened—they would see a good deal more of him now that he was back from the Smoke—soon got a job as a barman at the Fountain pub, Westgate Street, Gloucester, where Tom drank whenever he paid a visit to the city, just ten miles from Cheltenham.

****

Christine and Carter were sitting on a park bench in the Cathedral Gardens. It was a calm and peaceful day, sunny and mild—May at its best. Children, resplendent in King's School uniforms, were ambling by, in twos and threes, their satchels swung nonchalantly over their shoulders, the younger ones chattering nineteen to the dozen and laughing, the older ones silent and morose.

"What time do you think they will be here?" said Carter, looking up at the majestic cathedral tower with admiration.

Christine looked at her wristwatch and pulled a face. "Around two… almost that now, they shouldn't be long," she said, closing her eyes to the bright sun. "I wonder what this Frank Holroyd fellow is like," she trailed.

As if in answer to her question, Tom and Frank appeared at the gate to the path which surrounded the cathedral. Tom raised a hand in acknowledgement of the couple.

After the introductions, it was Frank who spoke first. "What is this then?—is it an interview for some newspaper story or merely just a friendly chat? If the former then I must insist that my name is kept out of all this. I must be anonymous. I have a wife and two children," he added for emphasis, looking directly into Christine's eyes. And she knew what he meant. She nodded and rested a hand on Frank's arm reassuringly.

"It is the former," she replied. "My editor wants me to do an in depth piece on Clean Oil Global, warts and all—and there are, I am sure you will agree, plenty of warts. But I can assure you that you will remain anonymous, you will not be named."

Frank returned Christine's gaze and he slowly nodded. He believed her.

After an hour, they stopped talking and Carter got up, stretched his arms into the air and walked a little way down the path to loosen up. Christine let out an audible sigh at what had just transpired and Frank chewed his lower lip, watching a quartet of King's School pupils running across the grass. Tom remained impassive, apart from breathing quite heavily.

The result of Frank's snooping while at Clean Oil Global was clear proof that the worldwide conglomerate had bribed major scientific establishments and governments to, in short, turn their backs, or tell outright lies, about carbonite and its alleged advantages. It was one of the biggest swindles of all time. And, in a series of mobile phone photographs, Frank had secured evidence of huge sums of money being paid to scientific establishments and governments to perpetuate the myth that carbonite was 'clean'. It was fraud on a gigantic scale. And, from a newspaper point of view, it was potential front-page dynamite.

After checking Frank's ID and his CV, Christine arranged to meet him in a couple of days' time to show him what she intended to write... and to buy him a drink. He had insisted on no payment but a drink was a drink, after all. The Sudeley Arms was the agreed meeting place.

All four, even Carter, were nervous of the enormity of what the retired police officer had discovered, of what Clean Oil Global were up to... of how Planet Earth was even more endangered.

****

Sir Jeremy Butcher looked long and hard at his star reporter and then he closed his eyes for a second. He pushed the story back to her—four A4 pages of typed prose—and rested his chin on his hands, elbows on the desk, wondering what to say. He smiled and shook his head in disbelief. Christine, sitting casually on a chair opposite him, waited impassively.

"Christine," he uttered her name slowly, "you are sure of this man, he is telling the truth, have you got any evidence that he is who he says he is... and that he has his facts right?"

Christine nodded and pushed a bulky A4 envelope across Sir Jeremy's desk. It contained written evidence that he had been a detective inspector, that he retired and drew a pension from the Force, that he was then employed as a security officer for Clean Oil Global and that he was made redundant recently from that role. The envelope also contained numerous photographs taken by Frank on his mobile phone of bank account credits for huge sums of money, debited from various Clean Oil Global accounts and credited to a variety of sources, including governments and scientific establishments worldwide. Sir Jeremy took half an hour to sift through the documents and photographs, after which he returned them to the envelope and handed it back to Christine, without a word but with the slight raising of his rather bushy, black eyebrows.

"You have done well, Christine, very well, and I am sure that you know how important this is," Sir Jeremy began, "but I must go to the board, you know that. We cannot print this story without their agreement. I am sure you understand that. The implications are huge," said Sir Jeremy, shaking his head. "Huge." And he gave her an imploring look. Christine merely shrugged, got up, flashed a fake smile and walked out of the room without a word.

Sir Jeremy reached for the telephone (an old-fashioned Bakelite beast) but changed his mind, replaced the receiver, opened his central desk drawer and fished out a red mobile phone. He put the phone to his left ear and waited. After about two minutes he sat up straight, cleared his throat and said, in almost a whisper: "Good morning, Prime Minister… it's Sir Jeremy of *The Times* here. Can I see you as soon as possible please—it's very important?"

There was a pause, Sir Jeremy nodded his head and said goodbye. In ten minutes' time, the phone rang and Sir Jeremy nodded again and said: "Thank you, Prime Minister. I will get a taxi to parliament straightaway." And he turned the phone off and returned it to the drawer. He then picked up the envelope Christine had handed him, put it in his briefcase, called for a taxi on his landline, swept back his hair and left the office.

Sir Jeremy walked into the Houses of Parliament and was almost immediately approached by a young man, suited and efficient and very smiley.

"You must be Sir Jeremy Butcher. Will you come with me? The prime minister is in a private office overlooking the Thames, or what's left of it."

The young man knocked sharply on a door and Ruth Suzman said: "Come in please. How nice to see you, Jeremy," Suzman began, shaking *The Times'* editor by the hand. "Go and sit over there and we can talk. No one is listening so feel free."

Sir Jeremy walked over to a large, oxblood-red Chesterfield sofa, waited for Suzman to join him and then sat down, rearranging the scatter cushions. The prime minister had walked over to a cabinet and said: "Whisky, isn't it? I've got a very good single malt."

Sir Jeremy nodded and smiled warmly. She remembered his favourite tipple and he was impressed. Suzman always did her homework. She poured him a large whisky, added three lumps of ice and a dash of water and took the thick and heavy crystal glass over to the coffee table in front of the sofa. Then she returned with a large glass of Sauvignon Blanc, *her* favourite tipple.

"So Jeremy, what is this all about? Must be pretty important. I'm all ears."

Sir Jeremy told her and then he pulled the brown envelope from his briefcase and put it on the coffee table in front of her. She picked it up, sifted through the contents, which included Christine's story, and settled back in the sofa to read. After an hour she returned the documents to the envelope, placed it carefully onto the coffee table and looked straight into Sir Jeremy's eyes. And she waited.

"No, no I'm not going to publish the story, at least not yet," he anticipated her question.

She smiled and said: "That's a relief. We are off the record, aren't we, Jeremy?" He nodded firmly and she continued: "Well then, okay. We have been closely watching Clean Oil Global for some time. And I mean closely. When we got into power they, of course, tried to woo us. Carbonite this and carbonite that. But we bided our time. We had to get government ready and we needed to feel comfortable before we started to make some tough decisions. We are almost ready to make them, almost. Clean Oil Global is at the heart of those decisions. But we are not ready quite yet..." she trailed.

"So when will you be ready, Prime Minister?" Sir Jeremy asked gently.

"Ruth, please," she chipped in, raising an admonishing finger. "I think that the time is almost here. Give us another couple of months. And then I shall get in touch with you and you can publish your story."

"Okay," said Sir Jeremy, getting to his feet and extending a hand. "That's a deal... Ruth... that's a deal."

8

The year is 2032 and the problem—a huge, worsening problem which is sweeping the world—is climate change or, to be more accurate, climate destruction. The human race is facing disaster, certain extinction, unless something is done immediately to reverse the trend. And this is global. It affects the whole planet and every living organism upon it. It is like a world war but in this case the enemy is us. We are committing suicide… and we know that we are. The enemy is our greed, our avarice, our determination to have more, quicker, better and with no consideration for the consequences. We now know what we are doing, we now know that we are destroying the very atmosphere that we need to survive but we keep on doing it. Governments throughout the world pay little more than lip service to the need to stop this. They hold conferences. Talk, talk and more talk…

But some countries—notably in the Middle East—could already see the writing on the wall: the days of oil were numbered. They had to think fast.

Saudi Arabia and other Middle Eastern countries had already unsuccessfully tried to woo many African countries into becoming markets for their oil with the incentive of cheaper vehicles for the masses. So an international cartel was formed with the intention of creating solar 'farms' throughout the deserts of northern Africa—millions of solar panels on the more stable stretches of the Sahara, the Great Western Desert, the deserts of northern Sudan, et al. The countries where it was intended to have these farms would be paid licence fees and the energy produced would be eventually sold worldwide. There were obviously huge problems to overcome in this undertaking—the biggest one being security—but, if handled carefully, the results could be beneficial to all—and to the planet!

While this was taking place, there was a general election in the UK and the old order—the tiresome, outdated order—became a thing of the past overnight. The Conservatives were decimated and the Labour Party was crushed. And the culprit? A new party called the Planet Earth Party (PEP for short, which the Red Tops press loved) who managed to secure 286 seats. The Tories won 202 seats, the Labour Party won 120 seats, the Liberal-Democrats got 10 seats and the Greens, independent and Irish votes accounted for the balance.

After days of backroom wheeling and dealing a coalition government was formed between the PEP, the Liberal-Democrats and the Greens. The political skyline was changed dramatically. The ridiculously outmoded battle between the Labour Party and the Conservatives was over. A new political era had dawned. The PEP was clearly in the lead, with help from the Liberal-Democrats and the Greens. King Charles was pleased with the result. Hugging trees and talking to flowers had not been such a bad mantra after all!

There was a lot to do and to do urgently. And this was a time for prioritising, for saving the planet at all costs. Several governments worldwide—including USA, China, Russia and India—had taken up the baton and had avowed to do whatever was necessary to save Planet Earth from self-destruction. It really was World War III. But there was one major obstacle which had to be overcome in order to begin to transform the landscape into a carbon emission-free zone. Despite the protestations and claims of Clean Oil Global, the worldwide conglomeration had to be stopped. Fossil fuels—and the drilling for oil—had to be consigned to the history books. And quickly.

So, for the next two years, not only was a new future mapped out globally (other governments had reached a similar conclusion) but work had already started on the transformation. Was it all too late? That was always the question hanging over everyone's head. Was it all too late? Nobody knew the answer of course, but the public had to be reassured, they had to play their part. But money and profit were no longer acceptable incentives. Greed had to be changed into caring—a Herculean task. But slowly people rose to the occasion. They realised that survival was the priority. A new mindset had been born. The world had to give it time to grow.

The UK government, led by Ruth Suzman, came to be in the forefront to the new approach. With the priority of survival above all else, the battle to save Planet Earth began. The sick and the elderly, the poor, destitute and homeless sector, the millions facing exclusion from society for any reason… they all had to take second place to the priority. As can be imagined this was not a very popular state of affairs. But it got the approval of the British people.

Ruth Suzman went to work. Her first target was the aviation industry, followed closely by the motor industry. A majority of U.K. airports—including Heathrow—were closed to tourists, amidst massive protest, and work began on building wind farms on the runways and concrete aprons. The target date for an all-electric motor industry was moved to 2035 but this time it was reinforced by government legislation. The writing on the wall was clear to see and Clean Oil Global was up in arms, but to no avail. There was no quarter. Clean Oil Global would have no customers in the U. K. after 2035. And many other countries followed suit so what the conglomerate did next was up to them… But in Great Britain they had just three years left.

It became mandatory for all new homes, offices, hospitals and factories to have solar panels installed commensurate with the numbers of people involved. And restrictions were lifted on all planning applications for solar panels on existing buildings. There was also a generous government grant, easily available, for the installation of solar panels.

The manufacture of wind turbines, solar panels and tidal barrages was—thanks to several years of scientific exploration—adapted to be carbon emission-free.

The major estuaries of the country—such as the River Severn and the Thames—would be adapted to provide onshore and offshore tidal power and there would be a proliferation of hydro-electric dams.

Such a massive about-turn in a bid to halt climate change came at a cost. And so the UK government levied a separate tax—the Energy Tax—on all taxpayers, across the board, of £25 per week. There were no exceptions. And, surprisingly, there was little protest. People, in the main, realised that this was vital, that this was a war, that the planet mattered more than individuals. The press was hugely instrumental in championing the cause, which soon became, quite rightly, the *raison d'etre*. It was fashionable to be *green*.

It was against this backdrop of monumental change that Ruth Suzman had to choose her timing of giving Sir Jeremy Butcher a telephone call regarding Christine's story about Clean Oil Global. She wanted to get the timing just right and so she waited. But time was not on anybody's side and she knew that only too well. And so, just two weeks after Sir Jeremy visited the prime minister and was asked to 'sit on' the story, she rang his private number.

Sir Jeremy answered the red mobile phone on his desk. He, of course, knew that it was her.

"Yes, Prime Minister, I agree," he said with a big smile on his face. But his voice was solemn. "In three days' time?" he said. "That's a Friday. It'll give Clean Oil Global the weekend to get their response ready. We'll carry their reaction in Monday's paper."

Ruth Suzman then warned Sir Jeremy of the predictable certainty that Clean Oil would institute legal proceedings against *The Times* but that she and the UK government would talk long and hard with the company. *The Times* was not alone, she reassured Sir Jeremy.

"You had better give Miss Jackson a few weeks leave, and quietly," suggested Suzman. "It would be best if she went away… in this country… and her whereabouts were not known. Clean Oil Global know how to fight dirty and I wouldn't want anything to happen to her."

Sir Jeremy nodded vigorously and turned off the phone. He put the mobile back in his desk drawer and leant back in his swivel chair, staring up at the ceiling. He then pushed himself forward, picked up the handset on his desk and asked the news editor and chief sub-editor to come to his office. Within a minute, they were both standing in front of him.

They sat down and read copies of Christine's story and looked at images taken by Frank Holroyd of various documents. It was a quarter of an hour before the news editor—a career journalist aged 56—spoke in a quiet but anxious tone.

"This is dynamite," he began. "You, sir, have picked a ruthless enemy and after Friday's story, they will be gunning for you, oh God they will. Have they any idea that this story exists?"

Sir Jeremy shook his head and shrugged his shoulders like a little boy caught out stealing sweets. "Not a clue," he said. "They haven't got a fucking clue."

When the two heads of department left the room, Sir Jeremy dialled Christine's number. She answered within seconds. He told her to take some leave—he recommended three weeks—and not to leave the country. She had to phone him every day. She agreed, turned off her mobile phone and turned to look Carter straight in the face, a huge grin on her face: "They are going to publish my story about Clean Oil Global. But Sir Jeremy wants me to go away for a bit."

"Can I come?" asked Carter softly, warming his hands around a mug of coffee.

She paused, put a forefinger to her lips and replied: "Of course, John. I can show you one of the most beautiful places on Earth—Salcombe, in South Devon, near the border with Cornwall. We can go on holiday!"

****

Two days later, they were aboard a train bound for Totnes, the nearest railway town to Salcombe. They sat opposite each other at a table seat and both looked out of the window, watching the 'green and pleasant' countryside roll by. They felt an enormous sense of relief. They were getting away… and nobody knew where they were going. At least, that is what they thought.

Christine leant across the table and put her hands over his, smiling into his face. Carter felt the love in her fingertips and he marvelled at the strange but wonderful feeling which invaded his being at her touch. This, he thought, was neither the mind nor the brain at work. It was something else. And he didn't know what it was. All he did know was that it was lovely and that he didn't want it to stop… ever.

At Exeter, a lot more passengers boarded the train. More and more people were holidaying at home now that a vast majority of the airports were closed and the warm weather— a bit too warm—was heralding the summer season. Carter looked up at the sun, through the window, and he pulled a face. It was burning hot, with the UV rays having less atmosphere to filter them. But the children in their carriage did not care about that. It was summer, it was hot and they were going on holiday… to the seaside. That was all that mattered. Carter watched them with warmth: they were young, they were excited, they were on the threshold of life, with all its problems ahead of them. For now it was holiday time. Carter felt a slow smile crinkle his lips and he shook his head vaguely.

At Dawlish Warren, the train curled around the coastline, very close to the sea, and to Dawlish, before heading slightly inland towards Newton Abbot and Totnes. It was a pretty route.

Carter and Christine and one or two others got off at Totnes and waited outside the station for a bus to Kingsbridge, about ten miles from Salcombe. They would have to wait at Kingsbridge for another bus to Salcombe itself. It was a difficult journey but it was worth it.

Once at Kingsbridge, Carter and Christine checked the bus times and then made a beeline for the Creek's End pub at the very head of the estuary. It was not really an estuary. It was a rhia—a virtually dried-up river outlet, one of only two of its kind in the country—and the tides played a major part in getting it well fed and alternatively drained everyday. It was fine at high tide but it was only just navigable at low tide. Getting stuck on barely visible mudflats was a constant problem. They had around an hour and a quarter to kill and the Creek's End was the best place to kill it in!

Thanks to a last-minute cancellation, Christine had managed to rent a two-bedroomed cottage in Salcombe, overlooking the church and Batson Creek. It had a terrace, outside table and chairs and a barbecue and was sheltered from the sun, which was fierce. It was only mid-May and it was already 26 degrees Celsius, but the sun's rays felt hotter, more direct, less filtered. Which they were. A depleted ozone layer was the reason but the human race was the culprit.

They lugged their suitcases, in Carter's case two bright red monstrosities, into the hallway of the cottage, dumped them and went back out onto the terrace, to soak up the lovely view. They sat around the garden table and Carter upturned his face to the sun, eyes closed and mouth slightly open.

"What shall we do this evening?" he suddenly asked, rocking back upright and opening his eyes.

"Don't let's eat in," replied Christine, shaking her head and then looking down at a gig, being rowed by eight women, arrowing across Batson Creek. Carter nodded.

"Where shall we go?" he said, following her eyes to the gig and then across at her.

"Ferry Inn," she said assertively. "And it's on me."

9

Conrad Stone checked into the Marine Hotel in Island Street, Salcombe, around two hours before Carter and Christine arrived in the town. He paid at reception for a three-night stay and went straight up to his room, not allowing a porter to carry his suitcase, which contained the usual items of clothing plus a high-powered rifle with telescopic sights, a silencer and a clip of bullets. He locked the door and placed the weapon, silencer and ammunition on the double bed. Stone spent some time assembling the rifle, checking the clip of ammunition and fitting the silencer. He then placed the equipment underneath the bed and lay down, staring at the ceiling with sightless eyes.

It was Thursday. *The Times* was due to publish Christine's story of the activities of Clean Oil Global next morning, but Stone did not know that. But what he did know, from his study of Christine Jackson's habits, was that she and that man she had with her were likely to take the ferry across to East Portlemouth in the morning, at around 10am. He could see the ferry landing jetty clearly from his bedroom window; he had a good line of vision, in other words fire, and tomorrow was his chosen day for earning a vast sum of money, enough to secure his retirement.

Stone had dinner and with it a half bottle of Cotes du Rhone and went back to his room. He got undressed and into bed and he was soon fast asleep. In the morning he opened the window and sat down on a chair, holding the loaded rifle… and he waited. It was eight o'clock and Stone yawned twice before settling down in the chair, looking out at the estuary where it narrowed to around 200 metres between the two sides—Salcombe town on one and East Portlemouth on the other.

****

At about the same time, Carter rose sleepily from the double bed, dressed and went down to the kitchen where he made two mugs of coffee. It was a lovely day so he took the mugs outside to the patio table, sat down and waited for Christine. She arrived, yawning widely, a few moments later.

"What are we going to do today?" asked Carter, looking down at two gigs, rowed side by side, crossing Batson Creek. There were hardly any boats moored in the creek, a huge difference from several years previously, when there were hundreds. But now there were a mere handful and the ones that were there were powered by electricity, not by petrol. The barge, moored in the centre of the estuary, now only dispensed electricity. The petrol pumps had long gone.

"I thought that we'd get the ferry across to East Portlemouth and walk along the cliff path to Gara Rock," said Christine. "I want to show you what Salcombe is doing to combat climate change."

They finished their coffee in comfortable silence, enjoying the early morning sunshine and then went inside, where they changed and walked up the steep flight of steps behind the cottage to the road. From there it was just less than a quarter of a mile down to Island Street and the Ferry Boat Inn, beside which was the jetty for the ferry across to East Portlemouth. The time was half-past nine. At 9.45, they were at the jetty and were waiting for the ferry, which had just disgorged its passengers at East Portlemouth and turned slowly around to make the return trip.

Conrad Stone, rifle at the ready, sat a yard from the open window and 'drew a bead' on Christine when his mobile phone rang. He knew that it must be Clean Oil and so he placed the rifle carefully on the floor, got up from the chair, walked quickly over to the coffee table in the middle of the room and picked up the mobile phone.

The voice on the phone said: "Project is postponed. I repeat the project is postponed. Please return to our offices straightaway. Telephone me when you are outside and I will arrange for you to be let in. If you need a reason for this last-minute change of plan, just buy a copy of today's *Times*. All will be explained." And then the caller (head of security at Clean Oil Global headquarters in Tilbury, East London) turned off the phone. Stone had not said a word.

Stone left the hotel, walked down Island Street to the newsagents, bought a copy of *The Times*, walked briskly back to the hotel and into the dining room for a late breakfast. It was 10 am. He gazed at the front page for a very long time before reading Christine's story.

CLEAN OIL GLOBAL CORRUPTION CLAIM, read the front-page banner headline, and below, a second deck, CARBONITE EXPOSED.

There was an Exclusive tagline, a picture of Christine and her byline and a cross-reference to a leader article by the editor, Sir Jeremy Butcher, on an inside page.

Stone read the front-page story and the leader article inside, folded the newspaper, placed it on a chair and waited for his scrambled eggs. He sipped at his orange juice and looked out of the window overlooking the estuary. He noticed the ferry boat, containing Christine and Carter, at the jetty at East Portlemouth, offloading its passengers. She had had a lucky escape, he thought ruefully, and, being the passionless man that he was, he thought no more about it. He enjoyed his scrambled eggs when they came.

Stone left the restaurant, went upstairs, packed his suitcase after dismantling the rifle, gave the room a cursory once-over and went down to reception. Half an hour later, he was in the back seat of a taxi bound for Totnes railway station.

****

Oblivious that she had been a couple of seconds away from a bullet in the back of the head, Christine clutched Carter's arm as the ferry boat sidled up to the jetty at East Portlemouth. They and the other passengers clambered out and trudged up the jetty to the road. They turned right and walked the length of the road to Mill Bay, where the road stopped abruptly. There they took the coastal path which wound its way up the other side of the bay, through a dense wood, and out into the open. Down below them, to the right, was the estuary and they could see North and South Sands and tiny Splat Cove over on the far side. Seagulls wheeled below them and waves broke over the Bar.

Christine pointed out the sights to him and said: "This is the most beautiful place on Earth. I have been coming here ever since I was aged about 12. It was always our holiday haunt. We went nowhere else. Why should we? It's all here."

Carter shaded his eyes to the glare of the sun and hunched his shoulders as he peered across the estuary to the other side.

"Wind turbines, there must be hundreds of them," he said. "And they are all painted green. They enhance the landscape rather than spoil it. What a good and simple idea. Green. They fit in with the countryside. What a good idea…" he trailed, shaking his head in admiration, and then striding up the steep coastal path, with Christine hurrying to keep up.

Christine stopped suddenly and pointed across the estuary.

"Bolt Head," she explained. "It's where the tidal power barrage begins. It was built right across the estuary two years ago, leaving that gap over there, marked by those two flags, for boats to pass through, mainly fishing boats. Doesn't do anything to spoil the beauty of this place, does it."

"Not like a factory belching out poisonous fumes, helping to destroy the ozone layer," said Carter softly but sadly. Christine looked at him and watched his back tenderly as he walked up the path. "Come on," he said without turning. She followed with a small smile on her face. She had found her man.

They reached Gara Rock and climbed the steep steps to the top where a restaurant and bar were situated. They sat near to the window which gave out onto the open sea, sparkling and twinkling in the sunlight. Two fishing boats, black silhouettes against the silver water, chugged by, en route to the gap in the barrage. They were clearly in no hurry, laden with their haul.

Carter took a sip of his lager and spoke, looking down into his drink: "That was a lovely walk. You are right. This is a beautiful place, it really is, and it is so good to see that the local populace are taking climate change seriously. It doesn't have to spoil anything, does it?"

Christine shook her head. "No, it really doesn't. Anyway, it's a small price to pay for the future of our planet."

They walked back to Mill Bay across the land, taking in buttercup fields, grazing cows and a myriad birds along the way. When they got to the stream which flowed through the forest to the bay itself and then across the beach to the sea, they took the wide, unmade path and walked easily slightly downhill.

At Mill Bay they were back on the tarmac road and they climbed up the hill and over to the ferry jetty where they were just in time to board the boat and chug back to Salcombe town. The tide was fully in and Carter looked across to the estuary mouth and the open sea, the sun on his face. He smiled a small smile of contentment and the offshore breeze ruffled his hair.

Walking down Island Street, hand in hand, Carter suddenly stopped and dived into a newsagents. He emerged a couple of minutes later, holding a copy of *The Times* and thrust it into Christine's face. She grimaced and closed her eyes.

"They might have told us it was today," whispered Carter crossly and the two hurried back to their cottage in silence.

****

Go Electric, heavily supported by Ruth Suzman and her government and endorsed by King Charles, had, for the past five years, manufactured some 20 million electric motor car batteries in its seven factories throughout the United Kingdom. It was working around the clock to achieve its target of 40 million batteries, a year or two before the 2035 watershed, when petrol-driven motor vehicles were to be banned. Needless to say they were not on Clean Oil Global's Christmas card list, not by a long way. Regardless of what the global conglomerate said or did to promote so-called carbon-free fuel the government was determined to achieve its goal: electric vehicles only on British roads on and after the year 2035.

The CEO of Go Electric was a far-sighted and charismatic 45-year-old by the name of Samuel Broadbent, who had launched the company only eight years beforehand. Broadbent, who had inherited his parents' millions, went to Oxford University where he gained a first class honours degree in electrical engineering. Having a visionary mentality, an eye on the changing times and an aptitude for hard work, he very soon found himself in a position to launch Go Electric.

After engineering a 'chance' meeting with Ruth Suzman at a business lunch, he formed a close relationship with the prime minister over the following few years, culminating in a lucrative contract to produce a majority of the electric batteries needed for the entire motor industry (which the government had nationalised).

Broadbent loathed Clean Oil Global with a vengeance but respected their power and ruthlessness. Although he kept them at arm's length, he watched their every move. And kept Suzman informed, of course.

When he read Christine's story in *The Times*, he immediately reached for his mobile phone, spoke rapidly, waited for several minutes and then said: "Ruth—it's Samuel Broadbent here. Have you seen the front page of *The Times*?"

10

Ruth Suzman was ushered into the studio and she sat down at a desk, opposite the camera. She extracted a sheaf of papers from her briefcase, placed them on the desk in front of her and looked up at the BBC presenter, who sat beside the camera. She didn't really need the papers; she knew what to say, off by heart... her heart.

"After a vote in the House of Commons last night, I am declaring a state of emergency for an indefinite period," she began, looking straight at the camera, in other words most living rooms of the United Kingdom. "Your lives will not be dramatically altered, don't worry, but I want you all to realise that we are now in a state of war—the Third World War—and the enemy is ourselves, us..."

Christine snuggled close to Carter on the sofa, in their rented cottage in Salcombe and she felt a warmth, from Suzman's words and from the man beside her. She felt elation and so did Carter, although he didn't understand what the emotion was all about.

Suzman carried on: "The deadline for an all-electric motor industry has been moved from 2040 to 2035 and you will be notified by your local councils within the next few weeks of what household goods are to be banned—the ones which damage our already badly depleted ozone layer. Hence global warming and, unless we do something about it now, we are facing extinction. Not just for us as human beings but for every living organism there is, from flies to elephants, and for the planet itself.

"We must act now to save our cherished planet, we must leave no stone unturned, we must put our beloved Earth ahead of all else. And that is why the United Kingdom, already in the forefront of the war against climate change, must make sacrifices for the common good. They won't be huge, I assure you of that, but there will be sacrifices, small ones…"

"She believes what she is saying," said Carter, sitting up and frowning. "She is not putting on an act, she is saying it as it is. And she is right, she is so right. It is such a relief to listen to an honest politician… at last. It is such a relief." Christine nodded deeply.

"It is time for all of us to explore our own country and to realise what a beautiful place it is," Suzman continued. "Because, fellow Islanders, you will not be able to fly away to exotic destinations anymore. The reason? Air travel will be restricted to essential journeys… and, I'm afraid to say, a foreign holiday by air is not an essential journey. So it is time to get to know your own country…"

Carter turned to Christine and said: "Places like here."

"Gas is to be a thing of the past and, I know, householders will be alarmed at this," Suzman said. "But electric boilers will take their place… and for the family this will be free. You will receive details from your own local councils, so you don't have to do anything.

"Please do not be alarmed by all of this. It requires a different mindset, a few adjustments, a realisation that what matters most is our survival, a new way of living, of being.

Please do not worry. We are going to win this Third World War, we really are!"

Ruth Suzman vanished from the screen. It had been a short speech but an impassioned and important one. Carter turned off the television and stood, legs apart, looking out of the window. A gig zig-zagged its way across Batson Creek, which was bathed in afternoon sun.

Christine's mobile phone rang—not a tune or a jingle but an old-fashioned, soft but urgent ring—and she answered it straightaway.

"Yes Sir Jeremy," she said. "Yes, I am fine… enjoying my holiday, despite the front page of the paper! I didn't know that you were going to print it when you did but I am glad that you did…" A pause, while she listened, and then: "Yes, yes, I was just watching her. Very good, wasn't it."

Christine was quiet for about five minutes, while Sir Jeremy spoke, and then she said: "That's fine, good idea. I'll come to the office in a couple of days' time and you can give me a full briefing. Ok?" She said goodbye and turned off the phone. She looked across at Carter, who was still standing by the window.

"Fancy a tour of Britain soon as we get back to Cheltenham?" she asked Carter with a smile and he raised his eyebrows and nodded vigorously.

****

The first thing Carter and Christine did when they got back to Cheltenham was to take a taxi to the Sudeley Arms pub, suitcases—one bright red one—and all. Tom was pleased to see them and the first drinks were on him.

The 'tour of Britain' was, in fact, to be a tour of green energy sites—solar, tidal, wind—throughout the country for a series of features which Christine was going to write. She was given three weeks. Sir Jeremy had told her to spare no expense and to get to work as soon as possible. The Times editor emailed her with a list of addresses she was to visit. He had already cleared them with the respective organisations. Christine excitedly told Carter all about it, over three large glasses of Merlot each.

"We are going to show the people of this country and the world what Britain is already doing to combat climate change," she said. "We are leading the field already and we want other countries—especially the USA, China and Russia—to follow our example."

"The Third World War has started," said Carter with a small smile and a large gulp of his wine. "But how are the articles that you write to be read by citizens of other countries?"

"Sir Jeremy has told me that he has struck deals with newspaper proprietors worldwide to run the series—my series—and so the Third World War has indeed started, John. Isn't it exciting?"

Tom ambled by and Christine stood up, took hold of both of his huge hands, stretched up on tiptoe (he was a very tall man) and kissed him on the cheek. He touched his cheek, smiled and said: "What's d'at for?"

"Thanks Tom… the story was down to you… so thanks!"

"The shit will hit d'fan now, though," Tom said. "Clean Oil Global must be furious. I would lay low, if I were you."

"Truth hurts, doesn't it," Christine replied. "About time they were told a few home truths, about time. By the way, Tom, how is Frank?"

Tom frowned and said: "He is scared shitless dat Clean Oil Global will know dat it was him. He's got a wife and two kids, so I can understand why he is so scared."

"Okay, but we will never reveal our sources—they will never get his name from us, Tom. You can reassure him of that."

Tom nodded, picked up some empty glasses and walked off, tea-towel over his shoulder. Christine took a sip of wine and said quietly to Carter: "Hope he's okay, Frank I mean."

Carter replied: "Clean Oil Global know that, from now on, they must be just that: clean. Squeaky clean. Their days are numbered, especially after Ruth Suzman's broadcast. They have only got three years left… to stop polluting the planet. I wonder what they will do…?" he trailed, rubbing his chin and smiling. He drained his glass of wine and stood up, stretching. Christine got up also and they left the pub, arm in arm, like some old, married couple. Tom smiled at their backs, but he didn't say anything.

****

Samuel Broadbent, his wife Madelaine and three children—John, aged 8, Jennifer, aged 6, and Sammy, aged 4—caught the train to Penzance for the first family holiday they had been on in seven years. They were going to board The Scillonian, bound for St Mary's on the Isles of Scilly, the following morning for two weeks, golden weeks as far as Samuel and Madelaine were concerned. They had booked a three-bedroomed apartment in Hugh Town, the tiny capital on St Mary's, and were looking forward to getting away from the stresses of running a big company, especially in such challenging times. The kids were just looking forward to the beach!

Go Electric, using cutting-edge new technology, were working flat out to meet the target of manufacturing 40 million batteries and to get them installed in new and existing vehicles by the year 2035. It was a tall order, a very tall one. But they were getting there and they had even inched ahead of the time estimate. The company, in its seven branches nationwide, were set to change the face of the motor industry in Britain for the future. But Samuel Broadbent, who had spearheaded Go Electric's lead in the national, let's say the global, race to get rid of fossil fuel consumption in all British vehicles, was worn out. He really needed this holiday and he needed it badly.

They reached Penzance, where the bumpers signalled the end of the line, literally, and they booked into a hotel in the centre of town. The following morning saw them board The Scillonian at approximately 9 am for the 26-mile crossing to the Isles of Scilly. The kids enjoyed scampering around the deck, while Samuel and Madelaine stretched out on sun-loungers, after thoroughly applying UV-block cream to their bodies. It was unwise to sunbathe without precautions: the depleted ozone layer allowed unhealthy ultraviolet rays to reach the Earth, often with very unpleasant consequences.

Samuel checked his mobile phone for messages. There were 14 but he resisted the temptation to open any of them. He needed the holiday and he needed to let go for a couple of weeks. So he turned off his phone and put it back in his shoulder bag, feeling quite pleased with himself. Madelaine smiled to herself and stretched over to squeeze his arm reassuringly. He knew what she meant.

The Broadbents moved into their rented apartment in the centre of Hugh Town at around midday, unpacked and settled in. With three bedrooms, a large living room, balcony with a table and chairs, well-equipped kitchen, large bathroom and separate shower cubicle, it was spacious, comfortable and homely. And it virtually overlooked the Mermaid public house, which itself had lovely views of the sea. It was ideal.

After an hour on the Town Beach, building sand castles and playing with the kids, the family rejoined to the Mermaid, where they sat around a round garden table on the terrace, which overlooked the harbour, ordered lunch and drinks.

When Samuel went to the bar to get another pint, he didn't pay any attention to the small, middle-aged man who stood at the other end of the bar, sipping a whisky and water. He had never seen the man before and as he didn't look very friendly, Samuel ignored him.

Conrad Stone was relieved. He didn't want any conversation either, although he knew that the other man was Samuel Broadbent, owner and CEO of Go Electric. He had photographs and a file of the man in his locked briefcase back in his hotel room.

Stone toyed with his whisky and reflected on the telephone conversation he had had earlier with the head of security at Clean Oil Global. Stone had been on the balcony of his hotel room, where the signal was better, and the conversation was one-sided; the head of security did most of the talking.

Afterwards, Stone slipped the mobile phone into the back pocket of his trousers, leant on the balcony balustrade, rubbed his chin, chewed his lower lip and looked sightlessly out to sea.

"It has to look like an accident," the head of security had said. "There must be no guns, bombs or knives or any weapons. It must look like an accident."

Stone finished his whisky, smiled crookedly at the happy Broadbent family out on the balcony of the Mermaid, slid off his barstool and left the pub.

11

Ruth Suzman was faced with a quandary. She had learned from reliable sources that the global solar industry (of which she was naturally a strong supporter) relied heavily on the mining of polysilicon in the Uyghur region of north-west China by suspected forced labour. Around 40 percent of the world's polysilicon mineral was in this region and it was vital for the production of solar panels, at the forefront of the world's battle to provide renewable energy for the future. And yet forced labour was unacceptable in normal conditions. But these were not normal conditions. So Suzman was faced with a quandary.

Her long-suffering husband Karl lay wide awake beside her in bed at Number Ten. He knew that she was awake but he hadn't said a word. They had spoken enough about polysilicon over dinner and he knew, from experience, that she would get little sleep that night. Because tomorrow was a big day.

Since the UK had become the world's leading light in the fight to curtail climate change, Suzman had found herself the commanding officer in this 'war'. Therefore television stations in the UK had begged her to update viewers on the latest stage of the war on a regular basis. She had agreed with the BBC to broadcast to the nation once every week for half an hour. And tomorrow was the day for her first broadcast. So she was understandably nervous as she was not sure how her views on the mining of polysilicon would go down. But she was determined to speak her mind.

Karl Suzman made her breakfast—Weetabix, scrambled egg on toast, coffee and orange juice (with a furtive dash of vodka)—which his wife wolfed down, noticing the vodka but choosing not to say anything about it, and lingered over her coffee.

"What do you think people will say?" she asked him in a voice like a little girl's. "Will they be angry, do you think?"

Karl shook his head and replied: "Just tell them the truth. Just tell them what the priorities are. Just be yourself, Ruth." He leant across the breakfast table and shoved a copy of *The Times* in front of her.

FORCED LABOUR OR NO FORCED LABOUR—WE MUST SURVIVE, read the front-page banner headline. She had had a long conversation with Sir Jeremy Butcher yesterday afternoon and given him an 'undisclosed leak'. It was a wise idea to get in first, so to speak, because tomorrow morning's press might not be so kind.

****

Christine Jackson walked into Sir Jeremy's expansive office and sat down at a chair in front of his desk—a mahogany splendour with a faded green leather top and nine drawers. The middle drawer was the most important one: it housed the editor's personal memorabilia. She smiled across the desk at her boss.

"Have you seen our front-page story?" Sir Jeremy asked, pushing a copy of the newspaper across his desk. It landed in Christine's lap. She nodded; of course, she had.

"Mrs Suzman is due to make her first regular weekly broadcast on climate change later this morning," said Sir Jeremy. "As you will have read, we are behind her every step of the way. Christine, I want you to be candid with me. Many action groups here and in other countries are outraged at the way the Chinese treat thousands of Uyghur people. They are, as you know, subject to forced labour in order to extract the mineral polysilicon to fuel a growing global market for the component which is used in the manufacture of solar panels.

"As you will have read, we, as a newspaper, support the need to manufacture more and more solar panels, at any cost, I'm afraid. And the cost is high; the cost is that forced labour, at this moment, is used to manufacture these panels. It won't always be the case, but for now it is. And so, we are, reluctantly, behind the Chinese, for the time being.

"What are the views of S.O.S. on this, Christine?"

Christine shifted in her chair and looked Sir Jeremy straight in the eyes. She closed hers for a second, heaved a huge sigh and said: "We have already met and discussed this—we held an emergency meeting—and we agree with you, Sir Jeremy. But, very much, for the time being. I must say that a worn and tired phrase leaps to mind: The End justifies the Means."

****

Ruth Suzman sat in front of the BBC camera, felt a fluttering nervousness in her stomach, closed her eyes for a brief second or two, looked down at the papers she had written, on the desk in front of her, cleared her throat and waited.

After a 10-9-8-7-6-5-4-3-2-1 from the cameraman, she began, suddenly feeling remarkably calm.

"Hello everyone. This is the first of a regular weekly update from your government upon the fight against climate change and we start with a growing crisis in the manufacture of solar panels, vital in our ongoing battle.

"The outrage at the exploitation by the Chinese government of the Uyghur people in the north-west of that country to mine polysilicon minerals for the solar panel industry worldwide is understandable. The much-persecuted Uyghur people are being used as forced labour, which is inhumane. We can only entreat the Chinese to pay these slaves a living wage.

"But we must remember our goal. We must save our planet. And solar energy is imperative in that fight. If we boycott the Chinese provision of the much-needed mineral and if other countries follow suit, then the only losers are us…"

Suzman continued in a similar vein for about ten minutes, speaking against a backdrop of clandestine video footage of the "enslaved Uyghurs" hard at work (in other words 'forced labour') mining for polysilicon in north-west China.

She ended the broadcast with the words: "We must always remember that our chief goal is to have a planet where we can all live. We must save the planet at all costs… however difficult that will be at times. But that must be our number one priority."

The prime minister's husband, Karl, was waiting for her in the carpark at Broadcasting House. She climbed wearily into the electric-powered Bentley and settled back in the front passenger seat, sunk or rather squirmed into the beige leather, opened her eyes, swivelled her head to look at Karl and said: "Let's go for a drink in a real, old-fashioned pub somewhere."

"I know just the place," said her husband and drove out of the carpark into a stream of traffic.

****

Carter and Christine caught the train to Chepstow at about the same time the prime minister was enjoying her first glass of red wine at Gordon's Wine Bar on the Thames Embankment. The pub—said to be the oldest wine bar in London, opening its doors in 1890—was situated underneath an underground line and the ceiling was domed stone, only about five foot six inches high in places, necessitating most people to crouch in order to get to the bar, which only served wine. It was a true wine bar. Every minute or so there would be a rumble above, as a tube train made its way somewhere. It was a wonderful place and Karl and Ruth loved it. It felt like drinking in a cave.

The journey to Chepstow was Christine's first in a series of countrywide trips to ascertain how the UK was doing in the field of renewable energy—the sun, wind and tides. Chepstow hosted the country's largest and most ambitious tidal barrage. It had been installed just two years ago across the River Severn estuary. And the trip from Cheltenham was not too long. Therefore, Christine and Carter were relaxed over their rather indifferent pizza, but rather splendid bottle of Merlot.

"There are a number of tidal barrages up and down the country," said Christine. "There is the one across the Thames, the much-smaller one we saw across the mouth of the estuary at Salcombe, one across the Clyde and several more across other river mouths."

Carter took a sip of wine, looked out of the window and said: "So, how long do you think we will be on this trip? Days, weeks or months?"

"I think about two weeks, give or take," Christine replied with a shrug. "But it's all on expenses so enjoy!"

"Does your editor know that I am accompanying you?" Carter asked with a frown, and Christine nodded.

They arrived in Chepstow railway station and were greeted by a downpour of rain the moment they stepped on to the platform.

"Global warming?" said Carter, with a grim smile as they huddled underneath an umbrella and made their way towards the taxi rank, which was outside the station. To their chagrin, there was a queue, but they had little choice.

****

After two weeks criss-crossing the country, Christine and Carter arrived at their final destination, which was home for the journalist. London and the tidal barrage across the Thames estuary. They booked into a hotel for three nights, long enough for Christine to get her story.

They lay in bed together, staring up at the ceiling and breathing heavily after their love-making. Carter was in a world of his own, perplexed but pleased with the sensations he was feeling, sensations he had never had before. What he didn't realise was that his mind had been invaded by Christine's and that a mystical thing called love had lodged itself there.

"I want to tell you some more about my second visit here, back 2,000 years, during the height of the Roman empire," he murmured, still looking up at the ceiling, his right arm draped around Christine's shoulder, his hand gently fondling her right breast.

"You mean when you were Jesus Christ," chipped in Christine, unsuccessfully stifling a chuckle.

Carter was not impressed but he carried on, although the fondling of Christine's right breast ended. Nevertheless, she snuggled closer to him and closed her eyes.

"The simple truth of the matter is that Christianity has been clouded by religious dogma," Carter began. "The facts are these: Mary gave birth prematurely to a baby boy in a stable in Bethlehem. There was no room at the inn because the little town was crowded with people embarked on a mission to register at a census, ordered by King Herod himself. The stable was the only vacant place for Mary and Joseph to spend the night.

"The Virgin Birth, the three kings, the star and so forth are simply part of the dogma. The truth is very simple… with just one added ingredient. Me, or rather my mind. Having a superior mind to the ones we planted in homo sapiens 200,000 years previously, I had little difficulty finding a host body for the job I had come to your planet to do: the creation of Christianity, as you call it, to replace the brutal and self-destructive order that was prevalent at the time. The Roman empire."

Christine turned on her side, facing Carter, and gently but firmly pulled his face around, so that he was looking at her. His eyes were unblinking, hers were hooded with perplexity.

"I find this hard to believe," she said, shaking her head. "But I know that you mean what you say… so I don't know what to think."

Christine paused, closed her eyes, regulated her breathing and then continued: "But I do think that I believe you. You are not mad, you are not delusional, but what you are saying is huge, it's mind-blowing."

"I know," conceded Carter. "I do really know… my love," he visibly recoiled at having uttered the endearment.

"What about all the terrible wars we have had?" Christine frowned. "The millions of men, women, children and elderly killed since the Roman empire collapsed. What about all of them? What about the First World War, the Second World War, the holocaust where eight million or so Jews were murdered for simply being Jewish? Why didn't you come back here then? Surely we needed to change."

"Yes, we knew all about this but we thought that the new mindset that we had installed would eventually come of age," Carter said with a mild shrug. "Basically, we held our breath because we were confident that eventually things would get better, which in a strange way, if you really think about it, they did… up until now."

Christine said softly: "But now you here again." She paused, chewed her lower lip and continued: "To create another new mindset?"

"No, not really, not now after what I have seen and heard," Carter mused enigmatically, smiled a small smile, turned and kissed Christine on the temple.

12

Samuel Broadbent toyed with his mug of coffee on the terrace of their apartment in Hugh Town on St Marys, the main island of the Scillies, and looked across at Madelaine, who was stirring hers.

"Would you mind if I went over to St Agnes on my own this morning and did a bit of walking?" he said and his wife looked up from her coffee and said: "No, of course not… you go and unwind and have a drink in the Turk's Head, which I know you will do."

Samuel leant over the terrace table and kissed his wife on the cheek. He then got to his feet.

"I'll pop down to the beach and play with the kids for a while and then I'll take the ferry boat to St Agnes," he said. "Goes at about ten," he added, looking at his wristwatch.

****

There were 12 passengers on the ferry boat—two families, Samuel Broadbent, a friend of the boatman and Conrad Stone. Stone was wearing sunglasses, a floral open-necked shirt and green Flash trainers. He looked nothing like the stranger Samuel had seen in the bar a day or so ago and he went unrecognised, not that it mattered but Stone was taking no chances.

The sea was quite rough and the little boat was tossed this way and that until they reached the island and the jetty which sloped upwards towards the Turks Head. Several smaller boats were moored alongside the jetty so the ferry boatman had to juggle for position. Which Samuel (being Samuel!) helped him with. The CEO of one of the biggest companies in the country clambered off the ferry boat and took the lanyard from the boatman, pulling the vessel around several others until he found a spot. The boatman thanked him profusely.

Samuel glanced at his watch—it was only 10.30am—so he resisted the temptation to go for a livener in the pub first and stoically embarked on his march around the island, which he knew from past visits. He took the rough, coastal path— and so did Stone, a couple of hundred yards behind. Stone walked slightly faster than Samuel, narrowing the gap between them.

The contract killer had visited the island the previous day and he knew exactly where to pounce. There was a very steep, grassy slope to the right of the coastal path, which led almost vertically down to a sheer cliff, which ended in a pile of boulders, slimy green from the sea. It was ideal—a perfect spot for an 'accident' to happen—and so Stone speeded up and narrowed the gap between him and Samuel to about 50 yards, fingering the heavy, round paper weight in the pocket of his jeans. He had rehearsed the incident at the spot he had chosen the previous day and in his head more than a hundred times since.

When Samuel reached the spot, Stone was just ten yards behind, walking on the grass by the side of the path so as not to alert the owner of Go Electric, who was lost in thought about his company's progress in manufacturing the battery order he had been given by Ruth Suzman, about the prime minister herself, about the climate change which threatened his beloved planet and about Planet Earth itself. He never heard Conrad Stone or suspected anything untoward.

After checking that the coast was clear—there was not a soul in sight—Stone hit Samuel hard on the back of the head with the paper weight, pushed him savagely on the left shoulder so that he fell down the grassy slope—rolling over and over—and finally over the edge, over the cliff and down to the boulders below. Stone checked again that the coast was clear and then he bottomed down the grassy slope until he got to around ten yards of the edge and got up slowly. He approached the edge cautiously and looked down to the bottom of the cliff, some 100 feet below.

Samuel Broadbent was spread-eagled across the boulders, a stain of blood oozing from his head, and he lay perfectly still. Stone looked down for a good ten minutes but there was no movement. Stone let out a grunt of satisfaction and proceeded to crawl back up the slope. Five minutes later, he was at the top and he surveyed the scene: he was completely alone. Brushing down his shirt and jeans, checking for blood, he turned and walked back down the coastal path, the way he had come, heading for the Turk's Head. He looked at his watch: a quarter to twelve. He would be at the jetty by around midday.

****

Samuel Broadbent was conscious when he fell over the

cliff and he desperately tried to grab the bushes which had boldly grown from the rocky cliff-face. Fortunately (it saved his life), he managed to grasp two bushes very close to the bottom of the cliff and his almost-certain fatal fall was broken. But that was not that all that was broken. So too was Samuel's spine, his right femur and his right forearm. And his skull was fractured by Stone's blow. But, totally conscious and in a lot of pain, he lay perfectly still, knowing that his assailant would want to inspect the result of his attack, hopefully from the top of the cliff and not from the rocky beach below. Which was exactly what happened.

After a quarter of an hour, Samuel raised his head, turned and looked up to the top of the cliff. The coast was clear. But try as he may, he could not move the lower half of his body. So he felt furiously in the pockets of his jeans and jacket for his mobile phone. Miraculously, apart from a cracked screen, it still worked. He phoned his wife.

"I've been hurt and cannot move." he began. "Someone cracked me on the head and pushed me over a cliff, where I am now, at the bottom, on a bed of boulders."

Madelaine, watching the children carefully and speaking so that they would not hear, whispered: "Where are you?" She added, pointlessly but understandably: "And lie still until help arrives."

Samuel told her and then flopped onto his back, the phone in his outstretched left hand, and lost consciousness. He only came to when he heard the guttural sound of a helicopter coming towards him. It was Air Ambulance, accompanied by a detective inspector. Samuel lifted his head and gave a slow wave with his left arm.

The helicopter hovered 10 feet above Samuel and then a ladder snaked down to the boulders. Two medics clambered down, gave Samuel a strong shot of morphine, strapped him carefully to a stretcher and got him up and inside the helicopter as gently as they could. Samuel bit his lower lip on one or two occasions, when the pain kicked in, but he didn't cry out, although he wanted to.

The helicopter flew straight to Penzance, where Samuel was admitted to the hospital. The detective inspector waited for two hours until a doctor came out of an intensive care ward and told him that it was okay for him to have five minutes with the patient. Through winces of pain, Samuel told the policeman the whole story and he explained who he was, at which the detective inspector raised his eyebrows but said nothing. Then, after a difficult few minutes, the owner of Go Electric fell silent and went to sleep.

Madelaine Broadbent arrived at the hospital three hours later, having left her bemused children being well-looked-after by the police in St Mary's.

****

Ruth Suzman put down the telephone and closed her eyes. The prime minister was shocked at the news but relieved that one of her favourite entrepreneurs was still alive. She made a snap decision, called her personal, private secretary to arrange transport, then security and finally called her husband Karl to tell him the news and that she was going to see Samuel. He understood… of course. And Ruth could not help thinking that she now had her material for the next Save the Planet broadcast, three days hence. She already had her suspicions—

and Clean Oil Global was top of the list—but she would have to be very, very careful about how she voiced them.

The following day, Ruth Suzman and two security guards (bodyguards, in other words) boarded a Cessna light aircraft bound for St Just Airport near Penzance. It was a warm and sunny late April/early May day, although the sun was hotter than it should be for that time of the year. The ultraviolet rays were not being filtered out sufficiently because the ozone layer was being depleted of its protective gases. It was a different, more fierce, kind of heat.

The prime minister looked up at the sun, her hand shading her eyes, and shivered at some ominous thoughts. But she said nothing.

After booking into a hotel, the bodyguards taking the room next-door to Ruth's, the trio visited the hospital, the prime minister acknowledging the waves and astonished expressions on people's faces on the way. She was not expected, but people were pleased to see her. She was a popular figure, a welcome breath of fresh air, of honesty. Especially after the last lot!

They found Samuel Broadbent sitting in a wheelchair next to his bed in a small, single ward, swamped in a blue, flannel dressing gown and reading a copy of *The Times*. He temporarily forgot and made to get up but, of course, he couldn't. He smiled an apologetic smile and patted the bed next to him. Ruth kissed him lightly on the cheek and sat down. The two bodyguards stood ramrod straight and unsmiling, with their backs to the wall.

"I am paralysed from the waist down—I will never walk again—or so they tell me," Samuel spoke with a radiant smile which clearly masked the agony he was beginning to feel inside.

Ruth approached him with a look of abject concern on her face. She placed her hands on both of his shoulders and kissed him again, this time on the forehead.

"Who did this?" she asked in a soft but angry voice.

Samuel shrugged and shook his head. "I don't know—it happened all so fast," he replied. "I only remember seeing, for just an instant, a floral shirt before I was knocked unconscious. But I have got my suspicions."

"Clean Oil Global," Ruth said through pursed lips, and Samuel nodded vaguely. The prime minister added: "I will see the police when I get back to London and we'll take it from there." There was a pause before: "They will pay for this… it is about time they were brought to book, it is about time."

"I would like you to know one thing, Ruth," started Samuel in a measured tone. "I may well be paralysed—I may well not be able to walk again—but I will work again, I will *really* work. I will leave not a stone unturned until you have your 40 million batteries… ahead of time. And I will use all my influence to, one, discredit Clean Oil Global, and two, get other countries, especially the main fossil fuel consumers such as the United States, to abandon oil in favour of electric." Samuel paused for a second, heaved his left shoulder (the right arm was very painful) and continued: "We *will* save our planet… it is worth saving."

The prime minster looked down at Samuel fondly, nodded, took a step forward and patted him on the left shoulder (she, of course, had noticed the bandages). "You are so right, Samuel, you are so right," she said, turned and left the room without another word. The two bodyguards marched off close behind her. Samuel watched them leave and slowly shook his head.

An honest politician at long last, he thought and closed his eyes briefly in contentment and admiration.

13

Christine Jackson sat rather primly in front of Sir Jeremy's desk, a notebook on her knees and a pen in her hand. She was ready for her orders! The editor of *The Times* leant back in his swivel chair, yawned, looked out of the window which gave out on to the street below and then in front of him at the hooded eyes of Winston Churchill in the portrait on the wall behind Christine. What would the savage old boy have made of things today, Sir Jeremy thought for the umpteenth time.

"Your pieces about tidal barrages made excellent reading, Christine," said Sir Jeremy. "Our readers loved them."

"So now it's wind farms," said Christine. "Might take me a bit longer, but I trust you are okay with that?"

Sir Jeremy pushed a thick file of papers across his desk and gave an apologetic shrug. "Of course I am, but you will be away for quite a long time. Oh, and that friend of yours, John, I think his name is, can accompany you… if you wish it and if he has got the time."

Christine sighed a small sigh of relief. "Thank you, boss. He would really like to come, I know it. And…" she opened the file and looked up at the editor, "My first call of duty is Staverton Airport, only a mile or so from where I live now. How convenient is that?"

Christine picked up the bulky file and her notebook,

nodded affectionately to Sir Jeremy and left the office to take up her next assignment. She felt excited and apprehensive at the same time, which was a good and useful mix of emotions to have for a journalist.

The following day, Christine and Carter took a taxi to Gloucestershire Airport (known colloquially as Staverton Airport, named after the parish it was situated in) and made a beeline for the Airport Inn, a good place to start their investigations. And, of course to have a drink or two, seeing that the 12 o'clock yard arm had just been exceeded—by about ten minutes!

They sat at the bar—much the way they had in London when they first met, some months ago—both turned to face the window which overlooked what used to be the runway, now festooned with 250 wind turbines, all painted green, and enjoyed the sense of peace and purpose which the revolving mini-windmills gave out.

Christine sipped at her glass of red wine and turned her head to look at Carter. "That is what it is all about," she added, stretching out her right arm at the window and at the wind turbines.

"Spoils the view, though," suggested a voice from the other side of the bar, a gentle female voice. It was the barmaid. "Used to be light aircraft—Cessnas and Partenavias and so on—coming in to land. Made a wonderful sight… when the runway was open, in the old days. They came straight towards you. Not so long ago though. Used to be a *proper* airport then. Not now, with that stuff over there, those wind turbines, hundreds of them, spoiling the view."

Gemma Miles stood behind the bar, shaking her head and absentmindedly wiping a beer pump with a grubby tea-towel.

But she was smiling, her eyes were kind, and she was pouting her lips at the memory. Despite what she had just said, Christine took an instant liking for her.

"Have you been here long?" asked *The Times* reporter and Gemma put a forefinger to her lips and closed her eyes for a second.

"I used to be an airhostess and I lost my job when my company went bust, couple of years ago," she started. "Badly missed flying and the first job was this one. Barmaid (full-time though) at the airport pub. It's not much but it just about pays the bills. Miss the planes though."

Christine kept her own counsel, raised her eyebrows, smiled warmly at Gemma, nodded and then turned to face Carter.

"The manager will meet us outside and give us a conducted tour," she said. "We've got about half an hour. Enough time for another drink?"

Carter nodded, turned back towards the bar but Gemma was already on the case. Two glasses of red wine were plonked on the counter within a couple of minutes.

The manager of the wind farm, a Daniel Brown, took them out onto the runway for a conducted tour. He explained the situation and the progress that had been made.

"The main problem that we all found in the field of wind turbine energy was the battery storage capacity," Brown said, as they wended their way between rows of revolving, green, metal windmills. "But Go Electric—you must have heard of them—came up with a battery that stored much more of the energy than before. It revolutionised the industry. A plant like this one can provide enough power—heating, lighting, cooking, etc.—for a small town. And there is absolutely no carbon footprint. It does no damage at all to the atmosphere and therefore to the planet. It's as green as it gets."

"Would you say that these batteries have transformed the industry?" asked Christine, who was busy scribbling into her shorthand notebook. "So, how many of these farms are there up and down the country?"

"I don't know the exact figure but I would say it has to be in the hundreds—they are everywhere. Not just on closed runways, but wherever you look. Wind power, with more than just a little help from Go Electric, has come of age. It really has…" Brown shook his head in appreciation of the company and then something suddenly struck him.

"You must have heard about Samuel Broadbent," he said, raising a forefinger in the air. "Such a shame what happened to him. Glad that he managed to escape with his life though. Were you anything to do with the story that I read?" the question to Christine.

"No, not really," said Christine. "*The Times* reporters who covered the story came to me, of course, to get as much information as they could on Go Electric. But I do know Samuel and he is the nicest of people, I can tell you. He won't let this get in the way of his goal."

"Which is?" asked Brown, inspecting a dial on one of the turbines.

"To see a totally green UK and ultimately a totally green planet… which is my goal too," she said, with quiet conviction in her voice.

"Mine too," murmured Carter, but nobody heard him.

****

Ruth Suzman sat defiantly bolt upright behind a little desk in front of a BBC camera, cleared her throat and waited for the green light. When it came on, she shifted her position. Elbows on the desk, she rested her chin on both hands and began: "I am assuming that you all know about the appalling incident on the Isles of Scilly a few days ago, involving one of our country's leading protagonists in the fight against climate change.

"Samuel Broadbent came just one inch away from losing his life, but he survived and now he is more determined than ever to play his part in saving this beloved planet of ours. The Earth.

"Although restricted by a wheelchair, it matters not. Because his mindset has only been strengthened by what has happened to him. Sadly, as there is an ongoing and thorough police investigation into the alleged 'accident', I can say very little. But those responsible for this attempt to kill the man at the top of Go Electric will certainly rue the day they ever crossed swords with the man. We, the government, will make sure of that. But I can send my, and I am sure, your sympathy and love to him, his wife Madelaine and their three children. And this I do, from the bottom of my heart…"

The prime minister then turned her attention to developments in global activities to combat climate change. The pace was hotting up and the new mindset was beginning to affect the way in which people thought and acted in what Suzman referred to as World War Three.

"Across the globe, solar and wind farms and tidal barrages are sprouting up," she went on. "Major former fossil fuel companies are switching to the green approach, implementing a change in mindset, by concentrating on renewable energy.

Oil—the dreaded carbon footprint—is becoming extinct, a thing of the past." She paused for a couple of seconds before continuing in a slow, almost pleading tone: "It is far better the extinction of oil than the extinction of Planet Earth.

"There are one or two exceptions to this, of course," she added, rather pointedly. "But if they don't all follow suit—and quickly—these companies will find themselves out on a limb. And facing collapse and ruin."

This barely veiled pointing of the finger at Clean Oil Global did not go unnoticed by the head of security and his cronies at the company's Tilbury headquarters. They were huddled around the television screen on the wall of the head's private office.

"We will hold an emergency meeting of the board next week, say 10 am on Tuesday," said the head of security and there was a buzz of agreement and excitement around the room. "The time has come for us to act, and to act decisively."

****

Christine Jackson and John Carter watched the prime minister's television broadcast in the bar of their hotel in the centre of Glasgow. Along with around 100 others. They had just visited one of the country's largest wind farms on the outskirts of the city—around 500 turbines, all painted green, of course—and Christine had, as usual, taken photographs on her mobile phone but also with the Nikon she had with her at all times. She was, as well as a talented writer, an accomplished photographer.

Carter seemed to be elsewhere. He was, as they put it, miles away. His eyes were half-closed, he was rubbing his chin and staring over the heads of the crowd, through the window. There was clearly something on his mind and Christine wanted to know what it was.

"What is the matter, John?" she asked in a small but insistent voice.

Carter paused for a couple of seconds before answering her. He put one elbow on the bar and turned to look her straight in the eyes.

"Suzman has made a very powerful and ruthless enemy today," he began. "It was obvious to me and therefore to most people watching that she has strong doubts about Clean Oil Global, that they are, in fact, responsible for the attack on Samuel Broadbent."

Carter closed his eyes for a second and shook his head slowly before continuing: "Clean Oil Global, as you know, are immensely powerful; they have factories all over the world and they make millions, billions, trillions of dollars and employ countless thousands of people. They are the biggest and most powerful company in the world, by far. For them to be accused of attempted murder, although thinly veiled, is a big thing, a very big thing, Christine. I think that Ruth Suzman, much as I admire the woman, has overstepped the mark this time. She has gone too far."

"But she is right," said Christine. "They were probably behind this attempt on Samuel Broadbent's life. She has only hinted at what probably happened. I don't think that she has overstepped the mark, I don't think that she has gone too far. I really don't."

Carter shrugged and opened his arms in supplication: "Okay, we must agree to disagree. But I am worried about this."

They finished their drinks in silence and left the bar, both deep in thought.

****

They caught the morning train from Glasgow to Birmingham, where they were due to get a connection to Cheltenham and (as an indulgence which Christine insisted upon) they travelled first class.

It was a lovely day—late May, a harbinger of the long, hot summer to come—and they watched Scotland turn into England and then the green, green grass of home flying silently by their window. Cows, in the fields below, turned up their heads to watch the train pass before continuing their constant grazing, the occasional swish of the tail, the occasional, unconscious flood of excrement, the very occasional stagger forward.

"Take care, I mean great care, won't you," said Carter suddenly and thrust his hand across the table between them, looking straight in her eyes pleadingly. "Because..." he lowered his voice, although they were alone in the carriage, "... because I love you."

14

At 10 am sharp on Tuesday of the following week, the directors of Clean Oil Global met at the company's headquarters in their converted warehouse at Tilbury in East London. It was a sombre affair. There were 12 directors present and some had come a long way for the meeting—from the United States, Canada, China, Brazil, Australia, India and South Africa. Europe was also represented by directors from France, Germany, Spain, Italy. And, of course, the United Kingdom.

The head of security introduced the chief executive officer of the whole conglomerate, Professor Donald Fortescue, a short and dapper character in his early fifties, with a balding head and a forever twitching, bird-like habit of jutting his chin this way and that. He was never still, never relaxed. He had very small, but penetrating eyes, set rather far apart.

Professor Fortescue began, with no welcoming preamble but straight down to business: "You all, I am sure, have heard about the unfortunate accident which befell Samuel Broadbent of Go Electric and his lucky escape with his life.

"But, more importantly, you will have heard and seen our prime minister on the television the other day when she gave her weekly climate change update. And the very clear inferences that in some way this whole sorry affair is our fault.

Our lawyers were very quick to utter a word of caution: in a nutshell they say that it is best to leave well alone. It will soon blow over and if we make a fuss now it will only draw attention to ourselves and the affair.

"So let's look to the future. The future," he paused, looked around the table where all the directors and the head of security were sitting and went on: "The future is, I am afraid, pretty bleak, well as far as the UK operation is concerned, very bleak. We have three years left, just three years before you will not be able to sell a single gallon of Clean Oil petrol at the pumps. Elsewhere in the world, the story is not anything like so bad. All the other countries where Clean Oil petrol is being sold are fine. They acknowledge the importance of carbonite. And they have carried out scientific tests on the ingredient and are satisfied that it eradicates the carbon footprint which used to be present in all oil-based fuels.

"So why is the UK government so inclined? Why does Great Britain have to stand up to the rest of the world? Why on earth does Clean Oil Global face such peril on these shores?

"I'll tell you why," the professor, clearly animated and angry, got to his feet, with both hands on the table, leant forwards and said: "The reason is simple, the reason is a woman by the name of Ruth Suzman. The prime minister of this country. That is the reason. Suzman is personally opposed to Clean Oil Global, that was obvious from her recent broadcast, and she has some notion that carbonite is not all that it appears to be."

There was a hum around the table, heads got together, there was a lot of nodding and opening of hands, there was a lot of agreement with their boss. One, the chief executive officer of Clean Oil Global's United States branch, stood up.

"Professor, we, on the other side of the Pond, totally agree with you," started Wayne Carlisle. "Laboratories and therefore scientists in New York state gave carbonite the all-clear two years ago. They say that it is totally clean. Totally. So what is all the fuss about over here?"

Professor Fortescue knew all about the scientific tests on carbonite in the United States. He should, because the conglomerate gave a multi-million pound donation to the scientific company, *with a few strings attached, of course.*

He shrugged and went on, sitting back down, as did Carlisle: "So the problem facing us today can be summed up in just one word. Suzman. Why she has got such a down on us, I do not know. But she has, oh yes, she really has."

The professor leant back in his chair, prised his hands together with his arms on the table and looked around the assembled directors with a satisfied expression.

The meeting continued for about an hour and the mood was clear: Ruth Suzman had to be persuaded, at all costs, to abandon her opposition to Clean Oil Global and reverse the legislation that all oil-based fuels should be banned as from 2035. That, it was decided, was number one priority for the company as a whole. Because the UK was the leading light in this area and other countries looked to Great Britain as an example.

The meeting ended, the waiters brought in trays of crystal glasses and decanters of whisky, the atmosphere became relaxed and the head of security even allowed himself a small drink as he chatted to Wayne Carlisle about American football (which he was a fan of, after spending a dozen years working in New York.)

After an hour and a half, everybody, except the professor and the head of security, went home, in jovial spirits thanks to the whisky. Two waitresses came into the top-storey boardroom and cleared the glasses. The professor and the head of security held on to theirs and stood together, looking out of the window at Tilbury Docks below. There was a silence for around five minutes before Professor Fortescue said: "What are we going to do, what the hell are we going to do?"

The head of security bit his lower lip, thought for a while and replied: "Suzman is a determined person. We have tried before, many times before, but she won't budge…" He paused for a while and then: "Her second-in-command is a get-rich-quick, career politician, with plenty of drive. Graham Southfield is a slave to hard work but he lacks commitment." There was another pause, a longer one than the first. "He is ideal," added the head of security quietly and the professor gave him a lingering, sideways look. The head of security turned and looked the professor straight in the eyes. "Without Suzman, the legislation can be reversed. Clean Oil Global, in the UK, can go on and on. Business as usual." He smiled a thin smile, without humour but with a lot of venom.

The professor nodded slowly. "She has made lots of enemies," he said. "Police wouldn't know where to start…"

The professor left the head of security alone in the boardroom and the first thing the latter did was to whip out his mobile phone and call a number.

"Send in Mister Stone," said the head of security and switched off the phone.

****

"It has never been done before in our entire history," said the head of security, treating Stone to a penetrating stare. "And you will never be able to work again. Once the job has been done then you will leave these shores for pastures new. And you will never return. Do you understand?"

Conrad Stone nodded slowly and returned the head of security's gaze. He felt both elated and daunted by the task ahead of him. Elated, because half a million quid was half a million quid, after all. He would not need to 'work', as the head of security put it, ever again. Daunted, because the assassination of a British prime minister was not a contract that came his way every day.

The head of security watched Stone's retreating back and ruminated: *He would not only leave these shores for pastures new, he would leave every shore and most certainly would not return*, he thought grimly, picking up his crystal whisky glass and polishing off what remained with one gulp. *We will make sure of that.*

The head of security sat down facing the window which overlooked Tilbury Docks. He stared unseeing at the grey water. It was gloves-off time, it was open war, he thought dispassionately. The only thing stopping Clean Oil Global from surviving and flourishing was in the shape of the prime minister of Britain, Ruth Suzman. She was a driven woman, a power to be reckoned with, but she was out on a limb. There was nobody else remotely able to take her place. With Suzman out of the way, the reversal of the legislation banning all carbon fuel, with or without carbonite, was an easy hurdle to conquer. And Clean Oil Global could continue to con the public and, in the process, carry on making billions of pounds and dollars all over the world, but, most importantly, all over the United Kingdom. The head of security allowed himself a thin, humourless smile.

****

Carter and Christine Jackson arrived back in Cheltenham, job done, after four weeks of training it the length and breadth of the country. Carter was seeing wind turbines in his sleep and he was greatly disturbed by the fact that he was having such vivid dreams: what the hell was happening to him? And Christine was just plain tired. She had filed her last piece—on the enormous wind farm on the outskirts of Glasgow—and was now looking forward to two weeks holiday.

"Could you drop us off at the Sudeley Arms pub in Pittville?" She leant forward in the taxi, fell back into the seat and grinned at Carter. "I think we both deserve a snifter… or two." Carter smiled crookedly.

When they got to the pub, they were greeted by Tom and Frank Holroyd. Apart from them, the place was empty, which was not surprising as the time was 4 o'clock in the afternoon. Tom nipped behind the bar and sorted out the drinks while Carter, Christine and Frank went over and sat down in the window seat. Frank, who was clearly nervous and apprehensive, said without preamble: "Has there been any reaction from Clean Oil Global to the story you wrote?"

Christine, somewhat surprised by Frank's direct approach, replied: "Apart from a front page devoted to their side of the story—along with two of their pet scientists' declaration that carbonite was as pure as the driven snow— apart from that, absolutely no reaction, which rather surprised

118

us all. Not a peep from their lawyers and we, especially my editor Sir Jeremy Butcher, expected there to be a furore."

"Sensible thing not to do," chipped in Carter. "As Christine explained to me a while ago, it's yesterday's news but today's fish and chip paper. Make a fuss and they keep it in the public eye; say next to nothing and it all goes away. As, for them, it has."

"So, what about the police investigations into the hotel fire, the bomb in Birmingham and the so-called accident to Samuel Broadbent of Go Electric? Have they come up with anything?" asked Frank with a frown. He had been a detective inspector for many years and if he was suspicious then so should they be.

"Not a dicky bird," said Christine. "*Ongoing inquiries* is all that we get whenever we ask. In other words, they haven't got a clue."

Frank pursed his lips, took a gulp of his beer, shook his head and looked out of the window reflectively. He stroked an imaginary beard and narrowed his eyes from the sunlight which poured into the room.

"Too damn quiet for my liking," he spoke to the window. "Clean Oil Global are up to something, I am sure of it. They are up to something."

15

Ruth Suzman and her husband, Karl, rented a four-bedroomed house in Vineyard Hill Road, Wimbledon Park. Although Number Ten was her official residence (and she spent a tokenistic amount of time in Downing Street), the house in Wimbledon Park was really where they lived. Much to the frustration of the civil servants and the prime minister's security team, who had begged her to base herself chiefly in Number Ten. But she would have none of it; she was that sort of person. Stubborn.

So, there was always a uniformed policeman a matter of yards from the house and a plain-clothed bodyguard in a car parked outside the premises. And the neighbours were fine about the situation. They were mainly students in flats or shared accommodation. And they were proud of having such a celebrity in their midst. And, more importantly, they, in the main, kept quiet about it.

Karl was a great tennis fan, so Wimbledon Park was an ideal location for him: he could walk to the All-England Club, especially at the end of June every year when two weeks were taken up with probably the most prestigious tennis tournament in the world.

The couple were frugal, down-to-earth people; not for them the trappings of wealth that so often came along with power. They had simple tastes (and very green ones too!) Holidays were spent in Scotland or Ireland, they dined in and Ruth did all the cooking but Karl always did the washing up and they occasionally had friends around for dinner. Once away from the hurly-burly of politics, Ruth led an ordinary life. On purpose. But they, or rather Karl, had just one exception. The white electrically-powered Bentley ever parked in the driveway. It was Karl's pride and joy.

Ruth ruefully wondered if he thought more of the car than he did of her, which was not the case. Nevertheless, he spent a good deal of time polishing the Bentley and sometimes just sitting in the comfortable, beige leather driving seat, fingering the shiny, polished mahogany steering wheel and sighing with pleasure. Ruth often found him there, at peace with the world, eyes closed, a smile on his face, 'away with the fairies', as some would put it. It was his (and Ruth's) one luxury.

Ruth was not the only one to find Karl asleep in his beloved Bentley. Conrad Stone, who had followed the couple home on occasion, also deduced that the Bentley was their pride and joy. He had seen Karl asleep in the driving seat of the car, parked in the drive, when he had 'casually' walked by. He correctly deduced that the car meant an awful lot to Ruth and Karl Suzman.

For four weeks, Stone had walked past the house and, of course, the car and he noted that Karl Suzman always spent a good couple of hours lavishing care on the vehicle the day before he was due to drive Ruth to BBC Broadcasting House for her weekly update on climate change. He always valeted the Bentley on Tuesdays.

Stone, who now rented a bedsit 100 metres up the road, knew that that was the day to make his move. He set about the subterfuge that would eventually lead to the assassination of the prime minister. He had a business card—a smart one—printed and it said: 'Exclusive car valeting service, inside and outside, at your own home. We come to you. Our rates are highly competitive and we provide the best service.' Stone leafleted the whole street, but with the intention of getting just one customer: Karl Suzman. Which he did.

Once a week, on the day before Karl took his wife to BBC Broadcasting House for her weekly update to the country, Stone spent two hours cleaning the Bentley inside and out. He was very thorough, trustworthy and punctual. Karl Suzman was well-pleased. For four weeks, Stone looked after the vehicle.

During his fifth visit, Stone slipped a parcel underneath the passenger seat. It was nine inches long, eight inches wide and three inches deep. It was a bomb with enough Semtex to reduce the Bentley and its occupants to ashes. The device was fitted with an electronic timer, which responded to a number which only Stone knew. He waited in his car, which was parked fifty yards down Vineyard Hill Road. The time was 11 o'clock and the Suzmans were due to leave at around midday.

At a quarter to 12, Karl and Ruth Suzman came out of their front door and climbed into the Bentley, which, of course, was gleaming. Karl drove slowly down Vineyard Hill Road towards the T-junction at the bottom. The car passed Stone, who was hiding behind an open copy of *The Sun* newspaper, and then, after 15 seconds, the contract killer entered the number and pressed 'call'.

The Bentley blew up a matter of yards from the junction and the prime minister of the United Kingdom and her husband died instantaneously in the explosion. One bystander, walking along the pavement, was cut by flying glass. The Bentley was reduced to an unrecognisable wreck of twisted metal and it was difficult to identify its occupants.

Stone quickly (but not too quickly) drove his car in the opposite direction and turned left at the top of the road. He parked again in a side street and kept his eyes on the rear-view mirror. And he waited.

The uniformed policeman and the plainclothes detective ran down to the Bentley, talking furiously into their mobile phones, and crowds began to form. The car was still burning and so they had to stand back. Hardly a word was spoken, apart from by the uniformed policeman, who assumed control of the situation. He told the thickening crowd to make way for the inevitable paramedics, fire and police, who, after his swift call, would soon be there.

The area was cordoned off, the crowds dispersed, hordes of uniformed policemen arrived, as did half a dozen members of the S.A.S. The press was not too far behind, although they were not allowed past the cordons. But from neighbouring properties, after much pleading, television cameramen got their pictures of the scene from top-floor windows. Albeit distant ones.

****

Sir Jeremy Butcher looked into the eyes of Winston Churchill in a painting on the wall opposite his desk. He felt numb. He felt empty. He felt desperately sad. All he could see, in his mind's eye, was the fiery, dedicated, driven and honest Ruth Suzman, a woman who he respected… and loved.

She was the only politician he had ever truly admired and trusted. And now, she was dead.

Sir Jeremy picked up the receiver of the old, Bakelite phone on his desk and asked his deputy editor, news editor and chief sub-editor to come in to his office. Within a couple of minutes, they were sitting in front of his desk, craning forwards, notebooks open and pens in hands. The expression on their faces was solemn. But through the despair, there was a strong sense of duty. They knew the enormity of the situation: the prime minister had been assassinated. This had never happened before. This tragedy was unique.

When they had finished, an hour and a half later, they scuttled out of Sir Jeremy's office and he phoned Christine Jackson. She answered straight away.

"I'm on my way," she said woodenly. "I'm on the train now—should be with you in about two hours." A long pause and then: "Are you okay?"

He shook his head and said: "No, I am not. I'm absolutely devastated. What a terrible thing to happen. But we must carry on, we must pay homage to possibly the best prime minister we have ever had." He looked at the portrait of Sir Winston Churchill opposite him and silently mouthed 'sorry'.

"See you later, Jeremy," she said solidly, showing the emotional strength of a woman and her editor welcomed the tone. He needed that strength more than ever before. Frankly, he needed her sitting in the chair on the opposite side of the desk, notebook open in hand and her eyes staring expectantly at him. He needed her there. Which, at 3 pm, she was.

"I passed Buckingham Palace on my way here and the flag was flying at half-mast," said Christine with a perplexed frown.

"Yes, King Charles ordered it," replied Sir Jeremy. "Only other time in history that it happened, apart from royal deaths, was when Princess Diana died in a car crash in Paris. And that was only at the strong suggestion by the then-prime minister, Tony Blair."

"So, what do you want me to do?" she asked, notebook open on her lap and biro in hand, awaiting orders. Christine was the consummate professional. The time for tears was later.

Leaving aside details of the assassination itself—that task had been assigned to others—Christine was responsible for the obituary, updated up until the present day. She had, of course, already amassed more than 2,000 words about Ruth Suzman, some time ago. She only needed to edit the existing copy and insert current details in her obit.

"What hat am I wearing?" she suddenly asked Sir Jeremy. "Your reporter or a member of the Save Our Souls action group?"

"Both," replied her editor without hesitation. "You are wearing both. I think the time has come…" he trailed with a shake of the head. "The time has come."

****

The funeral for Ruth and Karl Suzman was, at the king's gentle, backroom request, a state affair in Westminster Abbey. Besides members of the Suzman family and the royal family, including King Charles, many heads of state from all around the world were there as were celebrities from the worlds of music, television, films and theatre, business and politics and sport. There were several hundred invited guests and the abbey was full: every pew was crammed with mourners. A space had been left for Samuel Broadbent's wheelchair. His wife, Madelaine, and their children sat behind. Although a sombre occasion, it was a fitting and quite unforgettable day.

Sir Jeremy Butcher, a close friend of Ruth Suzman, headed towards the pulpit to make his speech. But he changed his mind, stopped en route, turned and walked down to the aisle. After five minutes of chaos as sound engineers moved a microphone in front of him, he began.

"I was originally going to say a few words to you about my dear friend from the pulpit—that was the plan—but on second thoughts, I thought that to be too condescending and not really appropriate so I am talking *with* you now… not down to you.

"I have known Karl and Ruth Suzman for many years and I am godfather to their first child, Tom, now aged 22 and at university studying biochemistry. I also know well their second child, Molly, now aged 20 and also at university, studying physics. They are both here today and they have my, and I'm sure, your deepest condolences for such a tragic loss.

"Ruth came to me a few years ago and told me that she was thinking of setting up a new political party. The name was to be the Planet Earth Party. She said that combating climate change was the only thing that mattered and that all else followed. She said that a different mindset among everybody was required, that it had to be in the forefront of people's thinking. She was impassioned beyond belief and also determined. Ruth was a trailblazer, a one-off, a person to be listened to. Which I did.

"PEP was duly formed and the rest, as they say, is history. She had reached a position which never could have been thought possible: the whole world admired and looked up to her. This country, thanks to her, now leads the way globally in the fight against climate change, the battle to save our planet—and therefore us—from extinction. We must make sure that we continue in the same vein.

"I will finish on one note, a rather sombre one, I'm afraid. Ruth Suzman was the first United Kingdom prime minister to be assassinated and I hope that she will be the last. But her legacy, her determination to put the survival of Planet Earth above all else, will live on. She was a true martyr to her beliefs. May she and her beloved and supportive husband, rest in peace. We must all ensure that this couple did not die in vain. Thank you."

Sir Jeremy, who had not looked at his notes once during his speech, turned and walked back to his seat. A single tear had rolled down his right cheek; he didn't attempt to brush it off.

The funeral was broadcast all over the world and an estimated four billion people watched it. There were many tears that rolled down many cheeks that day.

16

The police discovered a leaflet which Conrad Stone, masquerading as one Jim Rawlings, had posted through the Suzman's letterbox, offering his valeting services but the telephone number had been disconnected. They did, however, manage to establish that the late prime minister's Bentley had been cleaned every afternoon before the day of her broadcast for the past four weeks leading up to the assassination. But that was where the trail went cold. Stone had left the Vineyard Hill flat, which he had rented under the name of Rawlings, immediately after the bomb blast and driven down to Southampton, where he caught a cruise ship to New York.

But Conrad Stone was never seen again. In fact, he was poisoned aboard the ship and his body, heavily weighted down, was dumped in the Atlantic Ocean. Stone sank to the bottom of a very deep sea, a matter of miles from where the Titanic hit an iceberg and foundered many years beforehand. He had lots of dead companions.

****

Graham Southfield looked out of the window in Number Ten, Downing Street, and felt a panic attack coming on. He wanted this, oh yes, he had wanted this for the past 20 years, ever since he had entered politics as a 26-year-old. But not this way, not now, not under these circumstances. He had never felt more inadequate, more not-up-to-the-job, as he did now. But he was there and there was no altering that. He was there.

He had, of course, been to the funeral—he had even exchanged pleasantries with King Charles—but what stayed most in his mind were the words of Sir Jeremy Butcher. And he had seen the single tear roll down the cheek of the editor of *The Times*; he had seen the look on Sir Jeremy's face, the look of extreme sadness but there was something else. It was the passion in the man's voice. Sir Jeremy had obviously been inspired by Ruth Suzman and Southfield felt a strange stirring deep down in his own spirit. He closed his eyes and waited for the stirring to go, but it did not. In the matter of a few moments, he had caught the passion and he didn't try to fight it. Suddenly, being prime minister seemed to be his destiny; it was something that would grow and grow inside him. He felt the presence of Suzman, the passion of the woman, her belief. The mindset.

He switched on the intercom on his desk, leant forward and said: "Could you ask the editor of *The Times*, Sir Jeremy Butcher, to come to Number Ten sometime this afternoon?" He then sat back on his chair, rocking it until it nearly tipped over, closed his eyes and thought furiously: *What am I going to say to the man?*

Four hours later, Sir Jeremy was sitting opposite Southfield, who was behind his desk. The editor of *The Times* had a glass of single malt whisky in his left hand. He waited expectantly, uncertain as to why he had been so urgently summoned.

"You were a very good friend of Ruth Suzman, but you hardly know me," began Southfield. "I want to assure you that I intend to follow in her footsteps. I intend to lead by her example and I want you to be the first to know that. I would like to tell you of my intentions… but I need to know that I have got your full trust. Because most of what I am about to tell you is not for publication, at least not for now."

Sir Jeremy sipped at his whisky, coughed and said, in a quiet but forceful voice: "I understand, Prime Minster, I do understand. You have my word."

"I shall come straight to the point, Sir Jeremy," began Southfield. "I am shortly going to meet with Cabinet and we shall call a snap general election within the next three or four weeks. I feel and am only a caretaker prime minister and I wish to put my leadership of my party and therefore hopefully of the whole country in the hands of the people. I am sure that you understand that.

"Your speech at Ruth Suzman's funeral awoke a long-fomenting feeling in me," he continued, allowing himself a small but warm smile. "I realise now that a new mindset must be adopted, adopted by all of us. I agree with you, Sir Jeremy. We must put the protection and survival of our planet at the forefront of our minds. It must override all other considerations, all else. I am hoping that PEP will get back into power and that I will be able to carry forward Ruth Suzman's wish—and now *my* wish—to show the rest of the world what Green really means."

The editor of *The Times* shifted slightly in his chair, nodded his head and said: "I meant every word that I said. And if you follow her example, if you, as you say, show the rest of the world what Green really means, then you will have my and my newspaper's full support. On that you can count.

"How are you going to do that, how are you going to change the mindset of the people in, some might argue, so retrograde a way?" Sir Jeremy paused with his chin resting in one of his hands, narrowed his eyes and continued: "Because you know that we are talking about not only arresting climate change, but of uninventing the wheel, of going backwards. It is not enough to merely salvage what we can of the ozone layer. We must reverse the trend, rectify the damage we have already done, improve not just stabilise the ozone layer. If we are to survive, if this planet is to survive, then we must adopt a totally different mindset. We must put survival above all else. We really must, Prime Minister, we really must."

Southfield nodded gravely. "I am considering setting up a small body of people to meet and discuss climate change and what the world is doing about it. And this debate will be televised and shown live on the BBC once a week. That is why you are here. I would like to know if such a move has your blessing and therefore your agreement to publicise this weekly meeting in your newspaper. And there is one more thing…"

"The answer to this question is a resounding yes," said Sir Jeremy, without hesitation. "And what is the 'one more thing'?"

"I would like Christine Jackson to sit on this committee, in her role as a leading member of the Save Our Souls action group and not as a reporter for *The Times*. Would you also give *that* your blessing?"

Sir Jeremy nodded and said: "Of course, but you will have to ask her."

"I will, of course," replied Southfield, who already had.

Sir Jeremy left Number Ten, strolled along Downing Street and hailed a taxi, which took him across town to Gordon's Bar, the Suzmans' favourite watering hole, on the banks of the River Thames and underneath a busy underground line. He liked the bar and he fancied a glass or two of wine. He sat at a table beneath the vaulted, bare stone ceiling, nursing a large glass of Shiraz and listened, with faint amusement, to the rumbling of the tube trains above.

It had been a very good meeting, unexpected, to say the least. Graham Southfield was a changed man, mused the editor of *The Times*: he was no longer the career politician he had thought him to be, he was no longer a man driven by the lust for power. He had, in a very short time, become a man with a strong sense of purpose. He had become 'the man of the moment'. He had caught the fervour, the fever, almost the fanaticism… of combating climate change. He had changed his mindset.

Sir Jeremy felt an enormous relief and he closed his eyes as he reached for his wine glass. A tube train rattled overhead as the editor of *The Times* took a generous gulp of wine. *This is how things used to be*, he thought indulgently and a little inaccurately. *Before the advent of new technology, of artificial intelligence… of destroying our planet and all life living on it. This is how things used to be, but perhaps they can be again.*

Sir Jeremy walked to the bar and to another glass of wine. He had to stoop, to walk with a hunched back, as the ceiling was only 5ft and 6inches above him and he was 6ft and 2inches tall. But it was worth the discomfort. He ordered another drink and then he turned, with his back to the bar, and surveyed the scene. Apart from candles on tables and a smattering of wall lights, the room—which had no natural light—was dark and intimate. He loved the place.

****

The Climate Change Think Tank was formed the following week. The group consisted of Graham Southfield, Christine Jackson, Samuel Broadbent, Sir Jeremy Butcher and Professor Donald Fortescue. When asked about Professor Donald Fortescue a number of times, Southfield had replied simply (and honestly): '…it's good to have your friends close and your enemies even closer.' And so it was understood. Even by Broadbent, who had enough reason to despise Clean Oil Global.

The Gang of Five—as they soon became known as, especially by the 'Red Tops' press—met privately three times before they told the BBC that they were ready. And so the debates began. The viewing figures were impressive. Millions watched the often volatile meetings on Thursday evenings and surfed the Internet or read the newspapers the following day, where the events of the day before were scrutinised. And the international press also had a field day. The United Kingdom—a small island off the coast of France—had fast become a front-runner in the global race for climate change.

It kept Christine up in London for three days every week, much to Carter's chagrin, and to hers. But she caught the coach back to Cheltenham every Sunday and Carter was at Royal Well coach station to meet her every time… with a bunch of flowers, white lilies, her favourite.

"How did it go?" he asked her as they walked to the taxi rank.

"You tell me," she replied, hugging his arm. They walked down the Promenade, quite slowly, almost as one person. Carter smiled, looked down at the top of her head, gave her a kiss and smiled.

"It was good, it was very good. Every time Professor Fortescue opens his mouth, he drives another nail in the coffin of Clean Oil Global. It was wise of the prime minister to ask him to sit on the committee, very wise. It is just a matter of time before he caves in and toes the line, just a matter of time."

Christine shook her head and frowned. "But what can they do? How the hell do they ditch oil? How the hell can they be clean? How can they?"

"They buy up the companies producing solar, wind and tidal power," mused Carter, as they waited for a taxi. "They shut down Clean Oil Global, switch to renewable energy and, hey presto, they are still in business. They'll have to change their name, of course, but that's easy."

Half an hour later they were in the Sudeley Arms, with Tom as company and two glasses of Merlot in front of them.

"You looked good on the telly and what you had to say was pretty impressive," said the landlord of the pub, from behind the bar, a tea-towel over his shoulder and a hand on one of the beer pumps. He smiled warmly at one of his favourite locals. Christine put her head to one side and silently mouthed 'thank you'.

"Graham Southfield is going to make a special announcement on the telly tonight," she turned and spoke to Carter. "We mustn't miss it."

"At what time?" Carter asked.

"Nine o'clock on BBC1," replied Christine, and Carter
chewed his lower lip and inclined his head.

17

Carter and Christine sat on a settee in the living room of the flat in Pittville Lawn and watched the television set closely. It was five minutes to nine o'clock.

Graham Southfield's face swam into view and he wasn't smiling. He looked directly at the camera and began:

"I have just met with my Cabinet and a unanimous vote has been taken. I am merely your caretaker prime minister—I do not have your blessing—and so I will ask for it.

"In three weeks' time, there will be a general election and the principal issue is the survival of our planet and therefore us. The eyes of the rest of the world are already on us and in three weeks' time, they will be wide, wide open. Of that I can assure you.

"As your prime minister and leader of the Planet Earth Party, I will announce our mandate—which will be a simple one—in a few days' time. I am sure that the other parties contesting this general election will do the same.

"This is a short broadcast and I will finish by saying that you will hear many promises over the next few days, many pledges, but you will hear only one from us and that is survival, a change of ways, a different way of looking at things, a reversal of that old mindset which puts money and profit above all else. You will hear about a new mindset, a mindset which is essential if Planet Earth is going to survive. Thank you."

Carter got up, walked over to the television set and turned it off. He returned to his seat and leant back in the settee, turning his head and looking at Christine.

"He is a changed man," he said. "What he just said was from the heart. We have got a good one in Mister Graham Southfield. And I admire his courage. Going to the country now, with Suzman's assassination clouding the issue, is a brave thing to do. But I can understand why. He wants to lead for the people, but also *by* the people. He'll get my vote."

"And mine," said Christine. "I wonder if the BBC will still broadcast the Climate Change Think Tank or will they hold the debates back until after the election?"

As if in reply to her rhetorical question, Christine's mobile phone rang. It was Sir Jeremy and he told her that the debates were to be suspended until after the election. She told Carter.

"That means we've got time to take a holiday!" exclaimed Christine, smiling. "Let's go to Salcombe for a few days."

****

It was a gentle, warm late-June day, early morning, and Christine and Carter were sitting around the garden table, on the patio, overlooking Batson Creek. The creek was bathed in early morning sunlight and a couple of gigs were neck-and-neck on their way towards Salcombe town. One was rowed by women and the other by men. A few seagulls swooped and soared overhead, squalling to the world in general. Apart from that, it was totally silent.

Carter seemed to be internally debating something; he stroked his chin and frowned into the distance. After about ten minutes, he turned to Christine, looked at her for a long time and said: "I need to tell you the whole story. I need to tell you why I am here now. Is this a good time?"

Christine nodded slowly and rested a hand on his. They looked at each other and there was love in their eyes.

"We were like you," he began. "Like all on your planet, I mean. We had bodies, very similar to yours, if a bit shorter, but we had bodies. A couple of hundred thousand years ago. We came to Earth, my first visit, as I've told you, in space suits, from our own planet millions of miles away.

"We had ruined our own planet, we had destroyed it, just like you—not you individually—are destroying yours. We had ruined the atmosphere, which was much like your own, and we were facing extinction, just like you are today.

"But we advanced mentally and we had devised a way to escape our bodies and have only our minds. We narrowly escaped extinction. In the past 200,000 years, we became totally bodyless and presided over a barren and dead planet— killed by us, by our greed. But we survived, albeit as minds only, but without bodies, without brains, without emotions. It is a miserable existence and one that would go on forever. So we had to find a way out, a solution, an escape from what we had done to ourselves."

"Why haven't you been locked up?" Christine asked. "And why haven't I…because I believe you?"

Carter laughed. "I really don't know, my love, but I'm glad that we haven't been. Because every word I have said, and am going to say, is true."

Christine closed her eyes and slowly shook her head. "I know, but please go on."

"200,000 years ago approximately, we found your planet," Carter said. "It was very much like our own used to be, with very similar atmosphere, flora and fauna. There were, of course, slight differences but Planet Earth was what we were looking for. It was fine, it was fit for purpose.

"As I have said before, we chose your planet for an experiment. We wanted to see if the existing superior life forms—homo erectus—would respond to having minds as well as brains. We were on the point of losing our own bodies so we planted the seeds, or rather the minds, in existing bodies (as I have already told you) and then we waited."

"Until 2,000 years ago, when you came, or rather your mind did, to deal with the Roman empire… as Jesus Christ!" said Christine.

Carter smiled, raised his eyes, pursed his lips and continued: "Yes, that's right. And very soon afterwards Christianity was born. It caused a lot of problems but it solved an awful lot more: it rid the world of the Roman empire for a start. And that's got to be good."

"So what are you going to do now?" Christine asked. She shook back her long hair, turned her face up to the sun and then bowed her head to look into Carter's eyes.

Carter heaved a great sigh and then he said: "I will tell you, I promise, after the general election. But not until then." He snaked an arm across the table and stroked her on the bare shoulder. "But I think that I already know."

There was a pause and Christine suddenly got up, braced herself on the table, grinned broadly and said: "Let's have a picnic on the beach today. Let's catch the ferry across to East

Portlemouth and go to Sunny Cliff Cove, which we passed on our cliff walk last time we were here. Come on… we need to sort things out."

And so they did. Sitting in an old (but powered by electricity) boat—'Mary' it was called—Carter closed his eyes to the sunlight which bathed his face and savoured the feeling of pure delight which washed over him. He loved the fact that he could feel for the first time, that he could enjoy being alive, that he could love being in love. It was strange, because it had, for him, never happened before. It was a strange, new and beautiful emotion. Emotion, that was the thing. It needed a body and a brain and a mind, all in concert; it needed the combination… and it needed something else, some*body* else. For Carter, it needed Christine.

They walked to Sunny Cliff Cove, passing the head of Mill Bay and trekked uphill, along the narrow cliff walk, to a right turn, where they clambered down a steep, makeshift path and found a spot on the sheltered little beach, which was to be their home for the next hour or two.

Christine laid out a blanket and unpacked her rucksack, while Carter walked down to the water's edge and, barefoot, scuffed the surf, kicking the foam carelessly. He looked out at Splat Cove and South Sands on the opposite side of the estuary and, to his left, at Bolt Head, rugged and a little forbidding, overlooking the open sea. He felt the wind in his hair, the sun on his forehead and the cry of seagulls in his ears. He felt at peace, he felt…at home.

****

The first party political broadcast was on Tuesday of the following week. It was to be the mandate of the ruling party for the hoped-for next term. And it was delivered by Graham Southfield.

"The time for action—and sometimes it will be tough action—is now," started the prime minister. "We cannot wait and will not wait... the time is now. We must act straight away if we are to save our beloved planet and, with it, all the creatures, insects, birds and plant-life on it. And us.

"The eyes of the world are upon us. What we do will be followed all over this planet. We are being watched. And also we are being watched over by the late Ruth Suzman, sadly taken away from us recently. We owe it to her and to her memory and to her legacy, to carry forward her dream, her desire that Planet Earth will survive this, the biggest threat to our very existence. Us."

Southfield reinforced his government's pledge to drastically reduce carbon emissions and to artificially manufacture ozone, to be pumped into the atmosphere at specialist factories to be built all over the country. Work had already started on building these plants.

"What we are doing will be unpopular with many, but it is vital for our very survival," said the prime minister. "It requires a change in mindset. It needs you, the people, to do an about-turn, to turn your backs on profit, at any cost, and to build into your way of thinking that combating climate change must always be the first, and the most important, consideration. The future is yours, it is up to you."

18

Election fever gripped the country and was the topic on everyone's lips. People talked about it all the time, in the pubs, clubs, cafes, shops, parks and of course in their own homes. Especially after the assassination of Ruth Suzman and especially after the mandate announced by Graham Southfield on the television.

Christine had been summoned to London by Sir Jeremy, booked into a hotel near to *The Times*, and would remain there until after the election. There was a lot of work to be done, journalistic work. And so she took off her S.O.S. hat and replaced it with her journalistic one, for the next three weeks, until the election was over. She had a job to do.

Carter stayed in Cheltenham, regularly frequenting the Sudeley Arms, where he enjoyed the company of Tom, the landlord. The Irishman exuded warmth and good humour… and, strangely enough, wisdom. After all the madness surrounding the coming election, his presence was, for Carter, a welcome antidote.

"Who do you think will get in?" Carter asked Tom one lunchtime.

"The PEP… by a landslide," replied the landlord. "We must save our planet at all costs. And there will be costs…" trailed Tom, busy polishing a glass, with a tea-towel which had seen better days. "But anything beats extinction, doesn't it…except for a pint of Guinness!"

Carter laughed and pointed at his empty wine glass: "Or Merlot, Tom. Get me another one, old chap."

****

The Planet Earth Party romped home with a clear majority, helped by the Greens, not wishing to dilute the PEP agenda, who fielded fewer candidates than before. The Conservatives and Labour, bloodied at the previous election, were now humiliated and the Liberal-Democrats were nowhere to be seen. Graham Southfield had taken a gamble and it had paid off. He was the legitimate prime minister of the United Kingdom and he wasted no time in going to Buckingham Palace and telling King Charles that he was ready to form a government. The king was very pleased with the result, very pleased, and he told Southfield so.

A new mindset had emerged, especially amongst the young, whose future this was all about. The mindset was simple: put the planet first, profit a distant second. The survival of Planet Earth was vital and had to be considered before all else. It was the number one priority and capitalism had to adapt to that new way of thinking. Adapt or perish. It was as simple as that.

Carter bought *The Times* every day and read the newspaper from cover to cover; he paid special attention to all the articles written by Christine Jackson; and to the leaders penned by Sir Jeremy Butcher. There was also a down-page article about Clean Oil Global which caught his eye. The UK branch of the international company was planning to switch to the production of solar panels, wind turbines and tidal barrages and to rebrand itself as Clean *Energy* Global. It was to bid farewell to fossil fuels and planned to do so before the 2035 deadline imposed by the government. It remained to be seen if the rest of the global conglomerate would follow suit.

Christine returned to Cheltenham a week after the election and Sir Jeremy had given her three weeks' holiday, which she and Carter truly appreciated. It had been an exhausting time, but a satisfying one.

****

Samuel Broadbent was given a knighthood in the following New Year's Honours List. It was the first time King Charles had laid a sword on the shoulders of a man sitting in a wheelchair but they both laughed about the bizarre situation.

Go Electric met its target of 40 million batteries with time to spare and garages up and down the country swapped their fuel pumps for battery chargers. Petrol had become a thing of the past.

****

Carter and Christine were sitting at a table in the Sudeley Arms, near to a window which gave out on the street. It was a bright and breezy mid-September day.

"Well," began Christine, looking out of the window and not at Carter, "it's after the election now and I think that you have something to tell me."

Carter nodded slowly, leant back in his chair and said: "Yes, you would like to know why I have come back here this time? I will tell you.

"As I've told you before, 200,000 years ago, we planted minds in homo erectus in East Africa. They were the most advanced of any species on your planet at the time. Your scientists call the area we chose the Cradle of Mankind—near Lake Turkana, formerly known as Lake Rudoph in northern Kenya. Then, over the millennia, homo erectus started to migrate westwards and became, in your terminology, homo sapiens.

"And was born the Roman empire, which symbolised what homo sapiens had become—ruthless, cruel, barbaric. So my mind, as I have already told you, came again 2,000 years ago and found a host body."

"Baby Jesus," whispered Christine.

"You know all about that," said Carter. "But I have come again, in manufactured human form, and the reason is simple. It can be uttered in just two words: climate change.

"This is your biggest enemy and it threatens the very existence of your planet. Your greatest enemy is yourselves, the human race. But I think you already know that.

"I came here a third time to see if your planet would be a good place for me and my fellow minds back home to settle. You would not realise that we were here, do not worry; it would just be our minds, which would find host new-borns, like I did 2,000 years ago.

"We have only around two-and-a-half million minds—ours is a tiny, if dead, planet—and we wish no harm to anyone, no harm at all.

"Well, I have decided that Planet Earth would indeed be a good place for us. You have a beautiful world and I think that the global mindset has changed and changed for the better. The general election result in your country is evidence of that. And my travels for the past couple of years, all over the world, have shown to me that the human spirit is strong and that the mindset can be changed. So there we are," Carter said, smiling, and patted Christine on the hand. He reached for his glass of wine and was silent.

Christine whispered: "When do these two-and-a-half million minds plan to come to us? How will we know that they are here?"

Carter smiled again. "They are already here. All over the world… and they are waiting for their host bodies, as we speak."

"And you?"

"I am also already here… with you," he leaned forward and kissed her on the cheek, "and I'm staying."

End